Inward

Book 1 of Perception

by Rob Turner

This is a work of fiction. Names, characters, places, and incidents are the product of the author's imagination, or are used fictitiously

Published by Asgard Industries
asgardkernow@btinternet.com

" – so we end as we began,
With the man in the woman, and the woman in the
man."

Peter Gabriel, Blood of Eden

Perception: "(the) act or faculty of perceiving,
instinctive recognition of truth."

Pocket Oxford Dictionary, 1984

The *Perception* books have been a long time in the making. I would like to thank all those friends who have contributed invaluable feedback – you know who you are – and especially my brother Julian, and my wife Liz, for criticism and long term encouragement far beyond the call of duty.

One

There. Some hundred yards to the south of his normal landing place, the stump of a drowned building rose out of the water, about thirty yards offshore in the moonlight, what remained of its walls rising to perhaps twice the height of his boat's mast. The place he had explored when he first came here in the stolen canoe, thinking that it had to be safe. Almost noiselessly, the boat approached the gap where the long collapsed offshore wall had been. Max lowered the jib, and the boat, hardly moving now, glided into the flooded space made by the remaining three walls. The noise it made as it grated gently on the masonry seemed disturbingly loud.

Feeling the wall in the gloom, he was able to find a metal object to make fast to. Working as quietly as he could, he stowed the sails, checked again that his bow was to hand, and settled down to try to sleep. It was a long time coming, his mind preoccupied by the day's events and the unfamiliar sounds of water against wall, boat gently rubbing against wall on a slight swell. But time passed, and at length he slept.

When he awoke it was dawn. The light was strengthening, but the sun had not yet risen. He stowed his tools and enough food for the day in his pack, untied the ropes, and pushed the boat out into the morning, onto the now mirror smooth water. The awe he always experienced when entering the Ruins stole over him once again, born of the place's vastness and age, and the ever present fear that he might be watched by something hidden. He rowed as swiftly and quietly as possible across to the street where he normally landed. Rather than beaching the boat at the street's end as he sometimes did, he let it glide in behind a fringing wall. Cheek and hands lightly pressed against the wall, he steadied the boat, listening intently. All he could hear was birdsong. The moss on the wall was wet, the brick smelt of damp and age.

He pushed the boat into the angle between two walls with an oar, made it fast to a pair of rusted iron brackets. Shouldering his pack, he pulled himself up till he sat astride the wall. He sat immobile for a long time, intently scanning the shoreline, the nearer ruins, the street running away under the trees. Nowhere did anything move. Satisfied, he walked along the wall, dropped lightly down into the street just above the tideline. Again, he paused to listen.

The small cart he had brought on his previous visit was standing untouched around the corner, exactly where he had left it. The sun was rising across the Sound, throwing every detail of the forested Ruins into relief, bathing the world in rosy light. He could feel it warm on his back. He took the cart's handles in his hand, and set off up the gently sloping street, away from the water's edge.

The street was made of a smooth, greyish material, quite unlike anything he had ever seen before he came to this place. Though plants had spread across its surface over many years, it was still exposed in places, and larger trees had found it hard to become established except where the surface was broken, or against the buildings. The streets were therefore quite free of undergrowth, and the going, even with the cart, was relatively easy. He paused often, body tensed, looking about intently. Once there was a movement down the street, and he froze, but it was only a wild cat, immobile as he, looking at him from a distance. After a moment the animal turned, vanished into the ruins. At one point he went silently into a building to his left, emerging after a few moments with another reel of the copper wire he had found on his first visit, the copper he used back at the village to bend and grind into fish hooks, or cast into arrow heads. He put it in the cart, and took up the handles once more.

It only took him some ten minutes' walking to find the place. A long, low white building made of the same smooth material as the street, its top two floors had collapsed onto each other, leaving the basement intact. Wide ramps ran down to openings that he supposed might once have been closed by large doors. These had long since vanished, leaving openings through which the sunlight streamed in, dimly lighting the cavernous interior. He paused at the foot of the ramp, suddenly feeling small. Most of the buildings in his home village could easily have been fitted inside.

He put down the cart silently just inside the doorway, crouched down beside it, watching, listening for many minutes. Only the silence came back, overlaid by distant birdsong from the streets outside. When he was satisfied that he was alone, he took an arrow from his quiver and nocked it on the bowstring, then began to move further into the building, moving silently, poised on the balls of his feet.

The vast interior was divided up into lanes like miniature streets, by racks and shelves made of metal. Some of these had rusted and collapsed, blocking the aisles in places, strewing an incredible diversity of complex articles across the floor. Despite his need for haste, as usual he was unable to prevent himself putting the bow down, picking some of them up and turning them over in his hands, shaking his head in wonder at what the function of each might be. Many metal items were corroded out of all recognition, but some revealed fresh, smooth surfaces under a thick film of dirt, while others were lighter, apparently made of a material similar to the building's floor, or the tubing he had come to get.

It grew darker as he moved further into the building, but, as his eyes adapted to the gloom, there was still enough light to see. At length he rounded a corner, came upon the stack of drums that he remembered. Again he paused for a long moment and listened, then took off his pack, sat down, and spent a few minutes silently eating some food.

Breakfast finished, he took his measure from his pack, measured the diameter of the nearest drum. As he had thought, it was about six feet across, and there was no way it was going to go in the boat. He thought that the boat might take two drums' worth of tubing, if he could get it off the drum. He hesitated for a moment. Nothing for it but to do what he had planned, despite the risk. It should be safer to do the work near the entrance, where there was light, escape would be easier, and where he could be less easily surprised.

He shouldered the pack, replaced the arrow in the quiver, put the bow on his back. Then he took hold of the nearest drum, which was lying on its side, and strained to roll it upright. It was a little lighter than he had expected, and crashed over onto its rim, sending echoes rolling round the building. Max froze again, waiting immobile for several minutes, but could hear nothing as the echoes died away. He upended a second drum, pausing again. Then, with face set, eyes darting about, he began to roll the first towards the doorway, wincing at the noise it made.

It probably took little over five minutes to roll the two drums into the open door of a small room close to where he had left the cart, but to Max it felt like hours. Once the second drum was back on its side on the floor, he sat down heavily beside it, perspiring, heart pounding, listening. As he waited, the silence came back.

After a few moments he began to methodically unroll the tubing from the drum, pulling it into tighter coils which would fit in the boat, wiring it into place with twisted strands of the copper. When a coil got unmanageably large, he took out the small fine toothed saw which Oz had made for him over the winter, cut the tubing, and started another coil. He had just started rewinding the second drum when a sound outside made him freeze. Grabbing the bow and quiver, he was on his feet in an instant, looking out of the doorway, into the building. As he did, a small pig burst down the ramp and in at the main door, pursued by what seemed a shoal of cats. He heard a sound behind him and swivelled, as four more cats ran past him from one of the other doors. The pig hesitated momentarily, ran deeper into the building, pursed by the cats. Moments later an unpleasant noise went up from the gloom, followed immediately afterwards by silence.

Max exhaled once, then froze again. The shadow of a human figure had appeared in the sunlight striking in through the main door. Soundlessly, he moved back into the small room, cursing the signs of recent activity which littered the floor, his heart pounding. He nocked an arrow, pressed his body back against the wall, drew the bow and waited, every muscle in his body tense. For a moment time seemed to stand still, then someone stepped into the room and stood motionless, regarding him. His mouth opened in disbelief, as his mind assimilated what he saw. At last he let the bow drop. For a moment there was silence, then he said:

"Trudie."

"Max."

She flashed a hesitant glance at him. He had never seen her like this, wearing animal furs, long fair hair tied back, the skin of her legs stained from travelling. She carried a small pack, and her bow and quiver were on her back, as if she had known she wasn't in danger, or didn't care. Irrational anger flared in him, and he said:

"I almost killed you."

"Yes."

"Why didn't you say it was you?"

"I wasn't sure what you'd do."

"What are you doing here?"

"I come here, sometimes."

Again, although it was the last thing he wanted in the world, anger burned within him, at the unexpectedness of her, at this secret place not being secret any more.

"Don't be angry with me." Again the quick glance at his face, barely meeting his eyes. "I didn't mean to shock you."

"How do you know about this place?"

She hesitated.

"I knew you come here."

He shook his head, frowning.

"How could you know that?"

For answer, she simply looked at him, the blue of her eyes like the deep waters of the Sound.

"Don't worry," she said at length. "I'll never tell anyone."

"Why are you playing games with me?" he asked. "When one or both of us could have got hurt? When it's easy for you to run as fast as I can sail?"

"I thought you'd worry. I knew you'd seen me on the way, even if you didn't recognise me."

Of course. The running figure in the forest clearing as he'd sailed south, he thought stupidly, the climber on the crag up the coast. How could he have failed to recognise her? He had been so sure it was a stranger, a traveller, a man. He ought to have known from the way she climbed, but she looked so strange, so wild, standing here, the marks of leaf mould on her arms and legs, her cheek.

"I'm not playing games with you," she said. "I told you, I come here sometimes. But this time you were here." She looked away from him again, making patterns in the dust with the toe of her moccasin. "No one knows we come here. I wanted to talk."

"Why are you wearing furs? You look so different."

"They're better for travelling. Better in the rain. Warmer. Tougher. I keep them in a cave, and change clothes there. I couldn't wear these back in the village. I come into the forest for peace. It's better if no one notices."

He nodded slowly.

"Right."

Silence fell between them. Out in the gloom of the building behind him, he saw movement. One by one, the cats were coming out of the aisles, and he raised his bow again, but she motioned to him to lower it. In wonder, he watched as they came up to her, came around her ankles like a sea. She reached down to stroke their backs, their tails, an abstracted expression on her face.

"I didn't know you had cats."

"I don't. These live here. They help me when I come. It saves arrows."

"Wild cats don't come near people."

Again she met his eyes fleetingly, with a look that said she was used to being disbelieved.

"They help me."

He frowned, unable to argue. "I don't hunt here. I'm never sure if the animals are safe to eat."

"It's easier for you to carry things in the boat. I have to hunt as I travel. I just have to hope it's all right and I'm not in a place that's poisoned. But I know what you mean. I've seen things, here."

"What things?"

"Plants, animals, people, that don't look right."

"Like me, you mean?"

"I didn't mean that."

He put his bow down on the floor, then he said:

"You've seen people, here?"

"Yes." She gestured up the ramp behind her. "Miles away, over there."

"You must have gone further in than me."

She smiled a little, looking down at the ground again.

"You know what you're like. You can't walk past anything that interests you. You must get a bit distracted, here."

He grinned despite himself.

"That's true." After a pause, he went on: "Isn't it dangerous further in? If there are people?"

She shrugged.

"They never saw me. I know if someone's around."

He looked at her, trying to make sense of what she was saying.

"I was so careful, but you knew I was here." He hesitated, furrowing his brow. "Did you see me sail in, in the moonlight?"

"No. I didn't come down from the forest till after dawn. I usually go to ruins up there, on the hills, for things I want." She paused, then said, "Don't you remember, years ago, when my father whipped me? It was you found me then, up in the woods."

"Yes." He frowned, falling silent, remembering. Being drawn towards the forest by something inexplicable, wandering for hours knowing only that something was lost, until he came on her under a tree, her face buried in soft moss. He had known instantly who it was, only to be shocked by the dark stain that soaked the back of her blouse, by how still she lay. Relief had burst through him when she shuddered and groaned, as he finally dared to touch her. She was so cold. He had covered her with his clothes, had watched her eyes flicker open, had seen that she knew him. Had finally turned, as he knew he must, to her back. He had fetched river water to soak the fabric before trying to lift it, but he saw the tendons stand out in her arms, the way her fingers clenched in the moss, at every tiny movement he made. She never made a sound. He remembered his involuntary gasp, the mixture of nausea and despair, as he finally uncovered raw flesh. He had built a shelter over her out of branches and leaves, had lit a fire, gone to fetch more water and gather the different healing plants which, frowning, her face a mask of pain, she had tried to remember and describe. He remembered how he had made a preparation with the plants, and had dressed her wounds. And, months earlier, her pinched, ashen face at her mother's burial, the dead look in her eyes, the way she had stood with her arm around her sister's thin shoulders.

At last he said, "Why didn't you come in the boat with me, if you knew I come here?"

She sighed, shifted awkwardly.

"Lots of things. I told you, I go into the forest for peace." She was looking down at the floor again, tracing in the dust again with her toe. "Sometimes I just can't be round people any more, not even Tammi. There's no one in the forest."

"It's dangerous alone."

"I know if something's following me." There was a silence, then she went on: "I first found this place by accident, one time when I was just travelling around. Then I kept coming back because of the strangeness, because this place must be from before, and I was curious. And I found useful things." She looked around at Max's work on the floor of the room. "Just like you."

"This place is amazing," he said suddenly. "Just in here, there are thousands of things. It would take you years to understand what they were for."

"You're good at stuff like that. Those arrow heads you make are brilliant, really true. I don't lose nearly so many arrows now." She squatted down by his rolls of tubing. "What do you want this for?"

"I reckoned I could collect marsh gas from rotting waste, use it to heat things in the forge, instead of using charcoal." He could hardly believe she was interested. "Maybe even cook with it. This is to keep it in, to get it indoors."

She shook her head.

"I'd never have thought of that."

He watched her squatting there examining the tubing, her hair falling down her back, the cats about her feet. At last she said:

"Max, what do you think will happen to our village?"

"What do you mean?"

"There must be poison somewhere." She glanced up at him awkwardly. "So few children getting born. Problems when they do."

"I know," he said, with sudden bitterness, conscious of his dwarfism, of his unbroken voice. He felt awkward, angry again, because he was too afraid to tell her how he felt. Afraid of how she would react if he told her.

"Let me help you with this," she said suddenly.

He wanted to say that he needed no help, and he wanted her to help him. So he said nothing.

"It's a lot to do on your own," she said, "with the boat to load."

So they worked together for the next few minutes, saying little, he unrolling and cutting the tubing, she wiring it. Sometimes they came close as they worked, and he caught the scent of her, and sometimes their hands touched. Her skin was dry and cool, and he remembered how they had used to play together as children, how carefree they had seemed, before he became so conscious of his disability, before the world reached out and laid its hand on her. And he realised how little he had seen of her since then, since she had grown up, so that working with her now seemed wholly new. Looking back on that day, years later, he remembered his heartbeat, how his palms were moist, how hard he found it to believe that he could be so close to her, here on the edge of their world. He watched her strong, capable hands wiring the tubes, wondering that they belonged to the same hesitant, diffident girl who had come to the smithy that afternoon last autumn, to buy his arrow heads. Then it came to him that out here she could do and be what she pleased, that her survival in the forest was in no one's hands but her own, and suddenly he understood. He remembered seeing her running, on his way down the Sound, and he understood.

Soon the rolls were finished, and they carried them outside. The sunlight was blinding after the gloom of the building, and they could hardly see when they went back inside. They stacked the first few rolls on the cart, and piled the others up beside it. Max packed up his tools, and Trudie came outside again with him.

"Don't you need to go and get whatever you came for?" he asked.

"Let's finish this. Then I'll go."

"You're kind. You don't need to."

"You push the cart," she said. "I'll carry some of this."

She took a roll on each shoulder. He knew she did not mean to make him conscious of his limitations, perhaps had no idea that she did so. Then he realised that it was the contrast between the two of them that made him so aware of his shortcomings, that very beauty of her that drew him to her, and he smiled wryly to himself. They were both a little out of breath when they got to the shoreline. She laid down what she was carrying, they unloaded the cart, and went back into the Ruins for the rest. The remaining rolls went in the cart, and they took a handle each.

"This is a good little cart," she said.

"I found it broken behind Oz's shed the winter before last, and mended it. It's served me well down here. Bringing that first boatload of iron back for Oz without it nearly killed me."

He left her by the water, and went and got the boat, bringing it round to where the street ran down into the Sound. She helped him pull it up a little from the water, and together they loaded the piping. The rolls were bulky but not particularly heavy, and all but two of them went in. He tucked the cart out of sight, where he always left it, with the last two rolls in it. He went back to where she was standing in the sunlight, one hand on the boat, looking out over the Sound.

"Come back with me," he said.

She turned to face him.

"I have to go up to the high ruins," she said. "There's some things I need."

"Then I'll wait for you."

"Don't wait. Don't tempt fate. Remember the people, the ones I told you about."

"Then you shouldn't go up there."

"I'll be all right. I'll know if it's dangerous."

"I want to wait for you."

She smiled, looking away.

"You're kind to me, Max," she said, "but I'll be all right in the forest. I won't have very much to carry this time."

"Be careful, then." He got into the boat, realising that it was pointless to argue.

"I will. I'll see you soon, back at the village."

For a moment she stood holding the prow, her knuckles white as she gripped the wood.

"Thank you," he said. "I'm glad you found me here."

"I'm glad too."

She pushed the boat off. He waved once, then turned to hoist the sails. The boat heeled, turned, began to move out into the Sound in the morning sunshine. When he turned back she had gone with her cats, melted into the Ruins, but the look that had been in her eyes as she pushed him off would stay with him for hours.

Two porpoises joined him as he rounded the point, breasting the swells beside him as he ran before a brisk southerly breeze, with the sunlight dancing on the water.

Two

Max had been working throughout the morning in the yard behind the smithy, building the frame of his gas generator, a large box some seven feet square, out of close fitting planks. He had stopped work to eat some lunch with Oz, and now found himself unable to concentrate, back out in the yard. It was a typical early summer's day, cloud shadows chasing each other up the flanks of the hills, the temperature kept moderate by a breeze off the Sound. Frustrated, he put down his hammer and nails, and sat down in the shade at the back wall of the forge, hugging his knees. It was like having a headache, like having a thousand things on your mind at once. Images of the interior of Joss Taverner's barn kept coming into his head, Trudie's father's barn. He could see shafts of sunlight striking through cracks in a door, every detail of the dusty floor, to the smallest piece of last year's straw, but everything seemed oddly out of focus. He could understand Trudie being in his mind after the events of three days ago, but not these memories of the barn, which he had not been inside for years. He shook his head, but the images persisted. Abruptly, he got to his feet. There was nothing to be gained from sitting still when he was feeling like this, but he would have to be careful. Taverner's reputation for unfriendliness was well known.

Walking along the back of the smithy, he picked his way down alleyways for a couple of minutes. The Taverner farm was on the edge of the village, and by this route he would arrive at the large stone barn from the back. Two more minutes found him against its roughly mortared wall. Looking over his shoulder to check that he was unobserved, he moved carefully towards the end facing the Sound. He paused at the corner. Very quietly, barely audible above the sighing of the wind in the eaves, he could hear someone crying.

A door stood ajar as he rounded the corner, and silently he slipped inside, his eyes slowly adjusting to the gloom. Trudie was sitting in the middle of the floor in a patch of sunlight, staring sightlessly at the ground, her body racked by sobs. Tears stained her cheeks, and a livid bruise covered most of the side of her face. A flood of emotions welled up within him, so that for a moment he was unable to move, could just stand there in frozen silence. After what seemed an age, he walked silently across the dirt floor, squatted down beside her, gently put an arm around her shoulders.

"Trudie, it's me. Max."

She started at his touch, turned to look at him from red rimmed eyes, still overflowing with tears. He stroked her hair without knowing he was doing it, shaking his head wordlessly. After a long time he said:-

"What happened?"

She spoke so quietly he could hardly hear.

"My father."

Again, he shook his head.

"Why?"

"Because I went away. He said he needed me." She sighed, shuddering. "He said he'll kill me if I ever go away again. I don't think I can do this any more."

He had no idea what to say. Despair and frustration welled up in him. Through the tears, she said:

"I have to get away from here sometimes."

"I know."

She shook her head hopelessly.

"I don't know what I can do."

Slowly then, in that moment of stillness, coldness and disbelief began to wash into him, as a picture grew his mind of Trudie and her father together, of the man doing things to his daughter in the night. He recoiled from the image, squeezed his eyes tight shut, but it only grew clearer. Of course. Suddenly things made sense, and he cursed himself for his failure to see it for so long. Her reclusiveness since her mother died, the way she had turned in on herself as she grew, walling herself off from others, not even meeting their eyes. The jealousy with which the man guarded her, the risks she took in the forest. Of course. He squatted there, his arm about her shoulders, blinded by his own fury and pain. She drew away in his arms, and he looked up to find her watching him fearfully.

"Don't be angry with me."

"I can't help it." He could hardly trust himself to speak. "It's not you I'm angry with." Somehow he had to reach out to her, somehow try to touch her. "Trudie, I see it. I see it all, now. I know what's going on. I know what he does to you."

She looked up at him then, her face in the patch of sunlight, and he was shocked beyond words by the depths of shame and disgust which he saw in her eyes. The feelings seemed to invade his own mind too, and he pulled back from them despite himself, beginning to know the extent to which she felt herself devalued, soiled, degraded. He saw the certainty with which she knew that she would never be anything to anyone, except as an object, a thing to be used. He saw how certain she was that it was her fault, and how that would always trap her.

In that instant she sprang to her feet, crossed the floor, and was out of the door before he had time to move. Max's heart was racing as he got slowly to his feet. Overwhelmed by emotion, he knew that it was not him who she was rejecting when she ran, that she had never shared any of this with anyone, perhaps hardly even with herself, and had never intended to share it with him. He knew how unready she must be for this, wished he could be with her to help her with the pain, yet knew, at the same time, how much time and space she would need. He knew that he had no chance of catching her anyway. He had never felt so powerless in his life.

Hoping beyond words that she would be safe without her bow in the forest, that her disappearance and his part in it would not trigger another cycle of violence, he slipped out of the barn into the sunlight, walking as nonchalantly as he could away between the houses.

Stillness and silence in the silver night, save for the sounds of the river in the valley bottom, and the breeze moving in the dark forest beyond the fields. Only the moonlight, alike on the bordering oaks and the crag across the valley. Below, beyond the darkened village, the inky waters of the Sound stretched out beneath the eye of a near full moon, and far away in the night a wolf howled.

Trudie was crying very quietly, her mind still raw with the ragged edges of someone else's pain. Just now she had felt how it is to die, curled in a ball on her bed. All too fresh were the moonlight striking through the high pines, another awareness out there between the trees. A man, a traveller on his way from who knows where. She had felt the weariness in his legs, the stirring of hunger in his stomach, the scent of the pines in his nostrils, as he paused, his hand on the rough bark of a tree, looking for the best route between the moonlit trunks. She knew the distant sound of the river in his ears, felt the sigh of his breathing.

Then suddenly the soft sound of movement behind, the whirling with the heart in the mouth, to meet the yellow eyes of a wolf, silver grey in the moonlight. A wolf like nothing she had ever seen, half the height of a man. Too little time to reach for the bow, too little time even to move, the paralysis of fear as it lunged forward at him, the blaze of pain as the jaws closed on the throat. The icy douche of fear engulfing everything, the voiding of the bowels, the knowing that this was the end. The pain going on and on, as the animal flung him to the ground, shaking him, the tearing of flesh as consciousness ebbed away and the darkness closed in, until all she was left with was the memory of pain, incomprehensible in its immensity, filling her mind. Pain more vivid than the familiar furniture of her room, still lit by a single candle.

There was a noise in the passage outside, and her door opened with a slight creak. Fear cramped her stomach, as she looked up to see her father. He stood naked, with his coat about his shoulders, already aroused at the thought of her.

"You've been crying."

The familiar paralysis creeping through her, the passivity in the face of what she knew would come. But overlaying it, the death in the forest burning in her head. She could not answer him, with the nightmare filling her mind.

"Why can't you be happy for me, when you know what I like?"

"I'm sorry."

"Why can't you touch me, make an effort?"

She squeezed her eyes shut, shivered.

"I'm here. Won't that do?"

He let the coat slip from his shoulders, knelt down by the bed, reached out for her. She rolled onto her back, let her body unwind as he untied her nightdress, until she lay naked on the bed. She tried to relax, to slip away inside as she always did, as he ran his hands over her skin, her breasts, her thighs. But tonight something was wrong. Her mind still filled with nightmare, she lay under his hands like a dead thing, unable to make even the slightest response, to do even one of the things she had grimly taught herself to do, to try to keep him from Tammi. Her mind was far away under the high pines, her eyes unfocussed, and abruptly he stood up, eyes narrowed, and struck her a blinding blow across the face.

"I'll teach you to work harder, you little cow."

Two more blows followed, then suddenly she was being lifted by the shoulders and flung bodily across the room. Disorientated, she whirled round twice, crashed against the far wall, her head taking most of the force. The world seemed to swirl and grow dim. She could taste blood in her mouth, and slumped back against the wall. Perhaps this was the end, perhaps he would kill her this time. In two steps he was on her again, flinging her back on the bed. He took her then, forcing her legs apart and mounting her roughly, and she lay under him like a rag doll, broken, oblivious of the pain, uncaring whether she lived or died. It seemed an age until he burst inside her, moaned and rolled off her, got heavily to his feet. He blew out the candle, left without a word. Dimly, she was aware of the door closing.

She lay silently on her back for hours, naked, shivering, staring into the blackness with wide open eyes.

Max awoke early, from a fitful night's sleep. His head ached, the inside of his mouth was dry. He rolled from his makeshift bed in the corner of the smithy, and sat up, rubbing his eyes. Shafts of sunshine were streaming in through gaps in the shutters, striking through the dusty air. Birdsong was loud in the eaves.

He got up, stretched, stood still for a moment, frowning. Slowly, he pulled on his clothes, then went to the window and opened the shutters. Blinking at the brilliance of the morning, he breathed deeply several times, stretching again, running his hands through his hair. He went through the door into Oz's adjoining cottage, into the kitchen, had a drink of water from the jug, and took a loaf from the cupboard. Again he stopped, frowning, rubbing his temples, shaking his head. He hesitated, then after a moment picked up his pack and put the loaf in it. Back in the smithy again, he paused, as if as an afterthought, and reached for his quiver and bow. Then he quietly opened the door, let himself out into the morning.

The sun had just cleared the hills, and few people were about. Walking swiftly, wanting to remain unobserved, he made his way between the houses, towards the Taverner farm. Soon he was behind the barn again, listening. This time he could hear nothing but the birdsong, the distant sound of the river on its rapids. He sighed, frowned again, shook his head slightly. Still the feeling of deadness, of unease. Again he listened intently, then moved softly round the end of the barn. The door creaked noisily on its hinges.

Trudie was in there, sitting absolutely immobile on the floor. She did not move or react as he tiptoed across the floor, knelt down beside her, his eyes still adapting to the gloom. Her hair was down, like a curtain of gold about her face as she stared down at the floor, so that he could hardly see it. "Trudie."

She made no reply, sitting there in frozen stillness. "Trudie."

He touched her hand, and as he did so she shivered, once. Her hand was very cold. Hesitantly, he reached out and moved her hair back from her face, shock and incredulity flicking across his own as he did so.

"Oh, dear God. What has he done to you now?"

Both her cheeks were red and black with bruising, one eye was so swollen it would hardly open. Blood had dried on her face, where it had run from her nose and a gash on her temple. He could see bruises made by four fingers on the thinness of her bare upper arm. She turned and looked at him then, out of the blue of her one good eye, red rimmed from crying, a look that mixed shame and self loathing with fear, with wanting to run, with desperate need. He knew that she could not understand why he was there, that she was afraid, even of him, and suddenly he could hardly see her for tears.

Angrily, he wiped them away, watching a single tear roll down her own cheek.

"I'm sorry, Max."

Her voice was so quiet that he could hardly hear her.

"*You're* sorry?"

Huskily, she cleared her throat, shaking her head, and again her eyes filled with tears. Gently, he put an arm around her shoulder, took her hand in his.

"You're frozen."

"It doesn't matter."

"It does, to me."

"Why are you here?"

"How can I not be, now I know?"

She wiped her eyes, gingerly touching her temple.

"I don't deserve it."

"Why?" he asked. "This time?"

She shuddered.

"Max, I'm so ashamed. Ashamed that you know. Ashamed that I ran away from you."

"I'm the one who should be ashamed." He fumbled for the right words. "Because I didn't see what was happening for so long. Because it's me you're telling, and not someone else."

"There isn't anyone else. There shouldn't even be you." She stared at the straw and earth of the floor. "Why should you care about me?"

"I don't know. I suppose because of how you are." He fell silent, then he said: "Oz makes beautiful jewellery out of my copper, other people make clips for nets. What one person throws away, another will risk their life for. I don't know how else to say it. But I know you shouldn't be ashamed."

She sighed.

"I'm dirty. Worthless. Why should you care?"

He chuckled, bitterly.

"Look at me. Don't you think that helps me understand?"

"Oh, Max." She squeezed his hand, once.

"It doesn't matter about me," he said, hardly knowing what he was saying. "What I wish is that you could see what I see, when I look at you."

She shut her eyes then, raised her battered face, and suddenly the most astonishing wave of empathy washed between them that it left him feeling breathless, stunned. A tear ran from under her closed eyelid, and she smiled a little, shaking her head.

"I can," she whispered.

He was silent for what seemed an age, unable to speak.

"You *touched* me," he said at last, almost in awe. "Inside. Trudie, what did you just do?"

"I don't know. I just saw your care for me." She looked up, rubbing her eyes. "I know I don't deserve you, though. Saving my life after he whipped me. Being here now."

"You don't deserve to be hurt. Why? Why does he hurt you?"

"Something had just happened when he came. He likes me to concentrate. I couldn't, so he threw me against the wall."

There was a long silence, then he said:

"Does he usually hurt you?"

"Not like this, no. Not usually." She looked at him. "He'll hurt you, if he finds you here."

Again silence fell between them. She moved her cramped legs.

"What had just happened, when he came?" he asked at length.

She hesitated, as if wrestling with a difficult decision. Then abruptly she said:

"Come up into the forest with me."

"Why?"

"I need to show you something."

"People will see us. He'll find out."

She got painfully to her feet.

"I don't care. Max," she said with sudden entreaty, "I have to go up there to look at something."

"What?"

"I'll go anyway, but I'd rather you came too. For all sorts of reasons. It might be dangerous, and I trust you." She shot him an odd, piercing glance. "There's something I need to understand."

He looked at her.

"All right. Because I trust you, too."

"I need to get some things," she said. "I'll meet you at the pool above the falls, just inside the forest. I'll come up the river. You go a different way."

"All right." he hesitated. "Be careful."

"Go on. I'll see you by the pool."

He turned, without another word, and slipped out of the barn into the sunshine, made his way quickly between the houses, hoping, for her sake, that he was unobserved. He crossed the main street, nodding to the couple of people he passed, left the village by the southerly track that ran up between the fields to where the forest began. To his right, the waters of the Sound glittered in the morning sun. The track petered out under the first trees into three footpaths, and he took the left hand one, into the green spaces under the trees, taking his bow from his shoulder and an arrow between his fingers. Soon the path itself faded out to nothing.

He moved with the skill of the practised woodsman, stepping on nothing that would give his presence away, his eyes flickering over the forest floor, searching for movement between the more distant trees. Frequently he stopped to look behind him, or to listen intently, but the woods seemed empty of larger animal life. His fingers played with the flights of the arrow as he walked, watching the birds and a squirrel in the trees, putting aside the instinct of the hunter to lay some food by. The wind sighed in the leaves, sun flecks danced across the ground at his feet. In different times he would have enjoyed today.

Dropping down into a small valley, he scrambled up a crag amongst the trees on the other side, working his way round in a semicircle, aiming to keep the cultivated land well out of sight to his left. The ground fell away again, and he crossed a stream. Cresting the next rise, the rush of a larger river over rapids came to him on the breeze. In a few moments he could see it between the trees. He worked his way down the steep slope, and in a few more minutes came out into sunshine, the river at his feet. It danced over the rocks in the sunshine, throwing the light back at him. Just below the outcrop on which he stood, it lost itself in a deep, slow pool, in whose amber depths he could see fish moving, darting streaks of silver.

He moved downstream over the rocks, till he came to where the river threw itself into space over the fall, ribboning down into a chaos of spray thirty feet below. He settled himself on a ledge near the top of the crag by the falls, so that he could watch for her coming, and see whether she was followed.

Three

Within a few minutes he saw movement between the trees, saw her coming at her easy run up the grassy floodplain beside the river. She had tied her hair back, and had her pack and bow. As she neared the falls she had to scramble over outcrops of rock, and he remembered sitting in his boat down the Sound, watching a figure in furs climbing, it seemed so long ago. She passed out of his sight beneath him, at the foot of the crag, and he searched the lower valley intently. If anyone was following her, they were being very careful.

Moments later, she appeared at the other end of the ledge, as if she had known exactly where he was. She had washed the blood from her face, but the livid bruises on her cheeks and arms looked worse in the sunlight. He smiled, got to his feet, looked up at her face, gently touched the swelling round her eye. She was slightly out of breath.

"I look a mess, don't I?"

"A bit. Are you sure you're all right?"

She nodded.

"Won't he wonder where you are?"

"Probably not for hours. He's fencing, round by the crag."

She took a deep breath, hands on hips, holding her bruised face up to the sun, eyes closed. Then she looked down the valley, to the rooftops of the village nestling beside the river, next to the Sound. After a moment she turned back to him, lowering her eyes when she saw he was watching her.

"It's kind of you to come, Max. I feel better out here." She turned, looking up the valley. "We have to go up to the high woods."

He nodded, taking an arrow from its quiver, the bow in his hand.

"You lead. I'll watch behind."

They walked for almost an hour beside the fast flowing river, climbing all the time. They saw three deer, but otherwise the forest seemed deserted. Then, under a crag where a tributary joined the main torrent, they struck up the slope to the right. The oaks began to be replaced by pine and fir, the scent of pine filled the air. Max was blinded by sweat, his heart pounding, his lungs burning in his chest. Ahead of him, Trudie stopped suddenly.

"I'm sorry," she said. "I've been going too fast. You should have said."

Anger at his own inadequacy flooded him. It took him a moment or two to catch his breath.

"I didn't like to. I thought you'd be worrying about getting back."

"I'm sorry." She seemed preoccupied, only half aware of what he was saying. Abruptly, she turned, looked searchingly at him. "We're almost there now. Max, it could be dangerous. Keep your bow ready. I don't want to say any more. I want to see what you think."

Slowly, almost apprehensively it seemed to him, she set off again up the slope. Soon the ground, carpeted now with pine needles and heather, levelled off, dropped gently away to the right. There was a clearing there amongst the pines, a gentle depression floored with grass. Trudie approached it warily, skirting round it between the trees, and he followed.

"Yes," she said softly, half to herself. "Yes. This is the place."

She shouldered her bow, put her arrow back in its quiver, and stood for a long moment with fists clenched, looking into the clearing, as if lacking the courage to go further. Then slowly, a step at a time, she moved forward. Max followed a few steps behind her, arrow nocked and bow half drawn, watching her intently. Hesitantly, she walked across the clearing, towards a patch of flattened grass at the foot of a tree.

"Yes," she said again, almost in disbelief.

There had been a struggle in the grass here, he saw. Trudie bent, touched a dark patch at her feet, raised her fingers to her nose and sniffed.

"Blood," she said softly. "Clotted, but still wet." She turned to look at him, her eyes wide. "Max, this is the place. It was real."

"What place? What's real?"

"Where he was killed. The traveller."

"What traveller?"

She hardly heard him, shaking her head as if in wonder.

"It's real," she said. She turned to him, took both his hands in hers. "You can see it, Max, can't you? There was a struggle, in the grass, there. Something, someone's been killed here."

He nodded, disengaging his hands, looking at the ground.

"And been dragged off, this way." Fear suddenly knotted his stomach. "Wolf tracks. Look. They're huge."

She nodded, absently.

"Yes, I know."

"What do you mean, you know?" He shook his head, frowning, remembering. "You said it might be dangerous up here. Trudie, what's going on?"

She looked at him, her gaze flat.

"Last night," she said. "I told you I couldn't concentrate, when my father came. Before he came, I was out in the forest in my mind. I touched the mind of a traveller, up here, in the high woods. I was in his head as the wolf took him." Tears stood in her eyes at the memory of the pain, but she kept looking at him, her eyes fixed on his. "I needed to know if it was real."

"I've never seen wolf tracks this size," he said.

"Max." She took two steps towards him, put a hand on each of his where they held the bow and arrow. "Never mind the wolf tracks. Listen to what I'm saying."

"I am. How can you be out in the forest in your mind? Do you mean you were dreaming?"

"Are you dreaming now? Listen," she said passionately. "You've seen what I've seen, here. And that's not all. I found you in the ruins, I found you down by the Falls today. You saw how the cats help me. And then there's you. You found me after he whipped me, you found me in the barn. You knew about my father. No one ever told you." Her face softened. "I saw the way you see me, in the barn. You said I touched you. Remember." She looked into his eyes, her face full of entreaty. "Max, I can't explain this stuff. But don't try to tell me I'm dreaming it -"

She faltered, her voice trailing away, suddenly transfixed by the look of horror in his eyes.

"Run!" he screamed in her face.

Instinctively, she obeyed, springing to her right with all her natural athleticism, sprinting up the gentle slope, her bow falling from her back. Hearing nothing behind her, pausing after twenty yards to snatch a quick glance over her shoulder, to be stopped dead in shock at what she saw.

Max had not moved, he still stood where he had faced her a moment ago, holding his bow. But he must have dropped the arrow when she ran. Facing him, no more from fifteen paces from him, was a grey wolf, but no ordinary wolf, a wolf she knew, half the height of a man. Max's eyes were locked with the animal's, and neither moved. Fear clawed at her mind, screaming at her to run, but somehow she did not, because she had been in worse places than this.

She watched Max and the wolf. She could see how it would end. He would only have to move, and it would spring. He would have no time to take another arrow, nock it, draw

the bow. She looked desperately about her. Slowly,
deliberately, because she had no defence, she bent down,
picked up two rocks, was straightening up -

- as the wolf sprang at Max, jaws open, going for his
throat. She wanted to scream, but there was no time, no point.
As if in a dream, she watched him raise the bow at the last
moment, ram its end, with all his strength, down the animal's
throat. Then the wolf was on him, knocking him off balance,
and he was down on the ground, half under its body.

Trudie whimpered, hardly knowing what she was
doing, and ran back down the slope. She could see her bow
lying at the edge of the clearing. Too far. Ten feet from them,
she stopped. The wolf scrambled to its feet, making a
coughing sound, shaking its head, jaws open. Max rolled into
a crouching position, blood running down his face from a cut
on his forehead. Slowly, deliberately, she raised an arm and
flung a stone at the wolf with all her strength. It caught the
animal in the flanks. It yelped, and turned baleful yellow eyes
on her. Suddenly she felt naked, standing in front of it holding
nothing but the other stone. She could see blood oozing from
its nose. It took a step towards her, and behind it Max
suddenly moved in a stumbling run, making for her bow.
Distracted, the wolf whirled, and Trudie flung her second
stone. This time her aim was better, and it caught the wolf on
the side of its head, just below the ear. The enraged animal
turned back on her, as Max scrabbled for her bow, rolled into
a crouching position, took aim.

His aim was poor, and the arrow took the wolf in the
flanks. Again it turned back to Max, as he feverishly nocked
another arrow, drew the bow. This time the arrow found the
neck just below the jaw. The animal turned as if to run, took
two steps towards Trudie, then suddenly the strength seemed
to go from its front legs, and it fell forwards. The hindquarters
twitched spasmodically for a moment, it rolled over,
shivering. Slowly, as they watched, movement ceased.

Trudie felt faint, her heart was pounding in her ears. She realised her whole body was shaking. She closed her eyes, opened them again, walked unsteadily past the body of the wolf to where Max knelt motionless in the heather, bow on the ground in front of him, looking down at the ground. She squatted down beside him, put an arm round his shoulders. She could feel the knotted tension in his muscles. After a moment he exhaled shakily, lifted his eyes to look at her. The look in his eyes reminded her of the way her mother used to look at her.

"You saved my life," he said. "You had no weapons, you should have run."

She shook her head.

"I brought you here."

"You're amazing. The courage in you."

"Don't, Max." She shook her head again. "We did this together. We're still alive. That's all that matters." Gently, she touched his head with a fingertip. "Are you all right?"

He nodded.

"Have you ever heard of a wolf like this?"

"No. Nor one that hunts alone." She paused. "I wonder if there are others. I wonder if it waited for us."

"You said you'd seen things that weren't right, in the Ruins. Maybe it's poison. Maybe this is the same sort of thing. Something new. If it works it'll survive."

"Maybe." She stood up, picked up his bow from where it lay on the ground. It was intact apart from tooth marks, but the wolf's teeth had severed the string. Max was searching in his pack.

"I've got another."

He got painfully to his feet, leaned on the end of the bow to re-string it. She picked up the fallen arrow, pulled the others from the carcass of the wolf, wiping them on the grass.

"We ought to go back," she said. "But I want to show you one more thing on the way down."

"All right. But I've had enough excitement for one day."

She could not help smiling.

"It shouldn't be too exciting."

They retraced their steps, back over the hill, down the long slope into the river valley. He leading this time, she following, both with arrows nocked, never relaxing their vigilance. They talked little, each preoccupied with their own thoughts. About two miles above the Falls, Trudie crossed the river at a place where she could step between large boulders, and Max followed with difficulty, cursing his shorter legs. She led him up the other side of the valley under the trees, to a boulder field under a crag. Amongst the rocks, there was a cave, invisible from the lower slopes, and someone had built a quite elaborate shelter against its mouth. She looked at him.

"This is where I come," she said. "Where I keep what I can't take back to the village. I chose this side of the river in case they ever follow me with dogs."

He nodded, genuinely impressed.

"A lot of work, and well built." He ran his hands over the smooth translucent material that covered the timber frame. "What's this?"

"I got it in the Ruins. It's like the stuff your pipes are made with. It's waterproof. You can't tear it, but you can cut it." She pointed at a roll standing against the rock inside. "I've got more."

He looked into the cave, marvelling at the neatness with which everything was arranged. The furs she wore when travelling, the sheeting, a few cooking utensils, a roll of yellow rope, other small items which might have come from the Ruins. A spare bow and arrows.

"What's all this for?"

She grinned.

"Same as you. Might come in useful."

"Why have you brought me here, now?"

"There's nothing of mine, in the village. Only Tammi's seen this."

He nodded, slowly, understanding.

"Thank you for showing me."

"Are you hungry?" She touched her belly. "I didn't think of food. I had too much on my mind."

"I've got some bread."

They sat in the entrance to her shelter, side by side, sharing some of the bread. He needed time to assimilate the meaning of what had happened in the high woods, so he told her about the gas generator he was building behind the smithy, how he had worked out how to join the pipes, but couldn't think of a way to seal the generator box, make it gas tight. The waxed cloth he had been going to use would only rot, it had been a stupid idea. He fell silent, brows knitted.

"Why am I telling you all this, after everything that's happened? When you say there's nothing of yours in the village."

"There isn't, except for Tammi. But what you're doing's interesting."

Silence fell between them. At last she got slowly to her feet, looking out across the valley. "I should go back now, or he'll know. Then who knows where it'll end."

"Yes." Gently, he touched her hand. "I so wish there was more I could do."

She looked at him, the ghost of a smile on her bruised face.

"Killing the wolf will do for today."

"Be careful on your own," he said. "Just in case."

"I think it's all right," she said. "But I will be careful. And thank you for today."

Again, as their eyes met, he felt an echo of what had moved between them in the barn, that strange sensation which left him knowing that, with her, he had no need for words. They left in opposite directions, she heading down towards the Falls, he re-crossing the river by the way they had come, picking up and retracing his route back to the village. He moved as he always did in the forest, alert, poised, attentive, but inwardly his mind was preoccupied with the events of the past few days, as the images crowded in. He thought of her injured face held up to the sun, thought of her surrounded by cats in the Ruins, of the look in her eyes as she pushed his boat off, of the look he had seen on her face as she stood facing the wolf, holding only a single stone. Shaking his head in wonder, still awed by the strangeness, he remembered what had passed between them in the barn, and again just now, as they parted. He knew that she was all he had ever wanted, and that he had no idea where this would end.

Four

It was late afternoon, and Max was working in the smithy, joining a last length of pipe to the run. He had worked himself close to exhaustion, laying the pipe in a shallow trench from the generator in the yard. It had taken him far longer than he expected to knock through the footings of the smithy wall, then to lever up the flagstones and come across the floor to the forge itself. Now the choking fumes made when he joined the pipes with the hot iron were catching the back of his throat. Oz had worked around him with amused tolerance, unconvinced that the whole idea would work at all, but impressed enough by past form to put up with the mess and inconvenience. Now, the last joint made, Max slumped on a chair near the door, eyes closed, drinking water from a jug, while Oz poured copper from a crucible, casting another batch of arrow heads. The evening sunlight struck in through the open door, making slanting rays in the air, smoky from the forge.

A shadow fell across Max's face, and he looked up, squinting against the sun. Someone was standing in the doorway, holding a bundle. With a start, he recognised her, the way she stood. He stood up, the jug clattering onto the flags.

"Trudie."

Trudie, here. She came a couple of steps into the smithy, so that he could see her face. She spoke softly, as if not wanting Oz to hear.

"You look tired."

The unexpectedness of seeing her here left him almost speechless. He mumbled something about laying pipes all day.

"I brought you this," she said. "I remembered what you said about sealing your gas generator. I thought, if this is waterproof, maybe it's gas proof. And I know it doesn't rot, because of where I found it." She held out the bundle. "I don't know about joining it, but you said you can join the pipes."

He shook his head in amazement, smiling at her.

"Thank you. And for bringing it down for me."

"I hope it helps."

"Don't you need it?"

"I've got more," she said. "Remember." She turned, hesitantly. "I ought to go now. Be careful, Max."

Then she was gone, into the evening, leaving him holding the bundle of translucent sheeting. Preoccupied, he started when Oz spoke.

"She's a smart one." He chuckled. "I'll bet you hadn't thought of half that stuff yourself."

Max nodded, half to himself.

"No."

Putting down the empty crucible, Oz came over to him, rubbed the smooth surface of the sheeting between his finger and thumb.

"What is this stuff?"

"A bit like what the pipe's made of, I think." He hesitated. "She gets it from the same place."

"*She* gets it, eh? Herself?" He chuckled again. "Trudie Taverner, eh? Who would have thought it?"

"Thought what, Oz?"

"You and Trudie. You're a dark horse, Max, that's for sure."

"It's not like you think."

"You don't know what I think. You've had plenty of time to talk to her about marsh gas, that much I can see. Though God knows how, the way Taverner keeps her shut away."

Max looked down at the ground in embarrassment, and the smith's voice softened.

"Good on you, Max, that's what I say, however you do it. There's beauty and grace about her that you don't often see, and a good head on her shoulders. But you know as well as I do that Joss Taverner's a hard man, and there's not anyone, me included, who'd choose to take him on. You know as well as I do, he doesn't let her see anyone. Take advice. Be careful, if you're seeing her."

Max sighed.

"Some things you do because they make sense, some things you just do."

"I'm just saying Taverner keeps no counsel but his own, does whatever he likes. He knows no one's going to touch him."

"I owe you a lot, Oz. Putting up with me for years, taking me in when you had no debt to repay. I've been trying to pay you back in metal these last two years. This isn't like you think." He sighed, his dark eyes meeting the smith's grey ones. "You know the problems I've got, better than anyone. But I have been seeing her, to talk to. Down the Sound, miles away. Up in the high woods, yesterday. If I told you it all, you probably wouldn't believe half of it."

"Well." Oz stretched, hands on hips. "You can start, then, while I help you get this floor back down. I'm not getting up to this mess in the morning. Then you can finish telling me later, over some supper and some ale."

Max took the shovel and started to back fill the trench across the floor, while Oz compacted the soil with the sledgehammer, and then began to re-lay the flagstones. He told him the bald events, leaving out, of course, the details that he could not tell, of how her father shamed her, without which, really, his story was only half a story. They were bending over a flagstone, in a moment of silence, when a shadow filled the doorway.

"Joss Taverner," Oz said uncertainly, getting slowly to his feet, reaching for an iron that lay by the forge.

"My quarrel's not with you, Oz White," the man said roughly. "We've done business together over the years, and you've always kept your nose out of my affairs, unlike some. My business is with your dwarf here."

Ignoring the slight, Max moved round to the window, so the sun was no longer in his eyes, watching Taverner.

"You've been hanging round my daughter," the man said. "And been seen coming to my barn."

Max stood, arms by his sides, judging it better to remain silent.

"Nothing to say, I see." Taverner's eyes were narrowed, his voice low. "I've only one thing to say to you. You stop hanging about my daughter, dwarf. If I see you near her or my place again, I'll break your bloody neck. I'd do it now if your master wasn't here."

He turned on his heel and left the smithy. Loudly, in the silence, Oz put down the piece of iron he had been holding. Max was suddenly aware of his heartbeat.

"Like I said," muttered Oz. "Take advice."

"He doesn't know the half of it."

Oz shook his head.

"You better not tell me any more either," he said. "What I don't know I can't let slip."

They finished laying the floor in silence, each with his own thoughts.

Trudie was lying on her bed, drifting into sleep. Distantly, she was aware of drunken voices in the street, coming nearer. Her father had disappeared to the alehouse hours earlier. At least, she thought, if he had company, she should be safe tonight.

The voices passed close to her window. One of them was her father's, and there were at least two others.

"'S all right," she heard him say. "I'm telling you, 's all right."

The front door opened loudly, there was a bang as someone tripped on the step. The voices were in the hall. It would be all right, as long as they were with him. With luck he would have passed out by the time they left.

"Light a candle," he heard someone saying.

The voices were still in the hall. Then, with an icy douche of fear, of unbelief, she heard her own door being pushed open. She sat upright in the bed, clutching the covers about her. Her father stood, swaying a little, at the foot of the bed. Behind him she could see the broad shoulders of Stu Bell, the publican, and the tall, spare frame of Jez Yates, the miller, each as drunk as the others.

"Trudie." Her father put the candle down at the foot of the bed. "I been telling the boys about you. They reckon you're beautiful."

The impossibility, the shame, of these men being here in her bedroom, these men who she saw daily in the village. She said nothing, looking at them, her eyes huge in the candle light.

"They wondered how you are in bed. I said you'd show them."

She closed her eyes, shuddered, spoke almost inaudibly.

"No."

"Why not? You've no shame in showing me a good time."

"No. You can't mean it."

Yates had been hanging back near the other two, but now he peered at her face, frowning. She could smell beer.

"She *is* beautiful," he said, almost in wonder. He reached out his hand, gently touched her cheek, and she flinched. "But she's bruised. You knock her about, Joss?" He hesitated. "You said she'd be willing."

"She's willing enough."

"I don't like this," the miller said suddenly. "I don't like it being your daughter, and I don't like to think of her forced." He swayed on his feet.

"Not your problem," said Taverner. "She'll do the business with you."

"I don't like it."

Taverner swayed forward. In two swift movements, he pulled the covers from Trudie's grip, ripped her nightdress from her back. Eyes wide with fear, she pressed her legs together, clasped her arms about her breasts. Her hair fell about her shoulders.

"There," he said. "Still don't like it, Jez?"

"I like it all right." The miller's eyes narrowed. "But there's some things I won't stoop to, Joss Taverner. I'm out of here."

Taverner drew himself up.

"You'll go through with this, now you're here. Can't have you talking."

"I'm out of here," the miller repeated.

"You heard what I said."

Yates's fists balled at his side.

"Yes I heard what you said, and tonight I seen what you've done. Look at her sitting there like that. Ain't you got no respect for your own flesh and blood? You're shit, Joss Taverner, that's what you are, and you've fucked with this village long enough. Now you tell me to fuck with your own daughter so you can watch. You're sick, man, that's what you are."

Taverner swayed on his feet.

"No one calls me shit in my own house."

Bell elbowed the miller aside, sat down on the bed next to Trudie. She drew her knees up under her chin, moved away from him against the wall, like a cornered animal.

"Come on," said Bell. "Stop buggering about. You can see she's on for it." He ran his hand along her leg.

"Jesus," Yates said. He turned, stopped with his hand on the door. "I can't stop this, I can't take you both at once. But I don't want no part in this." He hesitated, and again his eyes narrowed. Then suddenly he turned back and swung at Taverner, catching him full in the face, with all his weight behind the punch. Caught off balance, the man went down against the wall, striking his head hard on the stone floor. He lay immobile, moaning slightly, blood leaking from his nose.

Bell was getting up off the bed as Yates turned to him, rubbing his knuckles.

"Now you, you dirty bastard," he said softly.

Bell faced the lighter man, arms loose at his sides. Suddenly he rushed at him, carrying the other against Trudie's dresser with a crack of breaking wood, pinning him against the wall. Yates smashed his forehead hard into the other's face, and, as he reeled back, dazed, his foot lashed out and caught Bell in the groin. The man doubled up, staggering.

In Trudie, crouched in the corner of the room, the fear and the shame seemed to break at once. She straightened her limbs, sprang from the bed, crossed the room and in a moment was out of the door. In blind panic, she struggled with the latch of the front door, then it gave, and blindly, unthinkingly, she was through the door, out on the main street, naked in the moonlight. She ran as she had run the night he had whipped her, ran from the shame and the humiliation, because anything, even death in the forest, was better than this. She ran, naked, barefoot, and empty handed, up the main street till it became a track, heading for the darker shadow that marked the beginning of the trees.

Max had been working for most of the morning in the yard, supervising the filling of the gas generator. He had made careful enquiries of the farmers, and the general view was that a mixture of compost and slurry rotted fastest. He had decided to layer the mixture. His initial attempts to barter copper wire for animal and plant waste caused great amusement, but they agreed readily enough once they saw he was serious, and a waggon of each from the Grant and Ridgeway farms respectively had duly arrived that morning. Transferring the slurry in particular had required buckets, an insensitive nose, and a sense of humour, but now the inner liner was almost full, and Max himself smelled almost as badly as the generator. Now, with Oz's help, he was up a step ladder welding the top seams closed with a hot iron, prior to weighting it to allow pressure to develop, and replacing the timber lid. A little experimenting on the sheeting had taught him how to make reliable welds: the crucial thing was the iron's temperature, neither too hot nor too cold.

They had just replaced the lid, and were leaning their elbows on it, chins cupped in their hands, enjoying the relative absence of odour and the cool breeze off the Sound. The two waggons had left the yard. Small white cumulus dotted the sky, cloud shadows chasing each other across the higher fields. As they stood there, a teenage girl came round the corner of the smithy, her blonde hair lifting on the wind.

"Max," she said. "Master White."

Max's eyes widened in surprise.

"Tammi."

He had seen much of Tammi as a child, when he and Trudie had played together, but since her mother's death and her father's increasing secretiveness, he had seldom met her. She had grown tall and slender like her sister, though still almost a head shorter than Trudie, and already more full breasted. The lips were thinner, the face perhaps a little finer featured, but the family resemblance was striking. So strange, he thought, to see her here now, so like her sister and yet so different, the way she levelly met his gaze, without the reserve, the sense of impermanence, the icy fragility of Trudie.

"What can we do for you, Tammi Taverner?" asked Oz.

"I came to ask Max, really," she said. "Have you seen Trudie?"

He frowned, shaking his head slowly.

"No." He paused. "Why ask me?"

She looked at him with her sister's eyes.

"I thought you might know. She told me how you saved her life."

Oz looked up at him sharply, and Max asked:-

"What's happened to her, Tammi?"

"I don't know. She disappeared in the night, three nights ago." The girl's face clouded. "She does go off on her own. She doesn't tell me about those times. But this time all her clothes are here, and her bow. I don't understand that."

"No." Max came down the stepladder. "Neither do I."

Tammi sighed.

"You've been kind to her, Max. She told me." She looked at him. "I expect she'll be all right. She always has been before."

"I hope so. I'll keep my eyes and ears open."

"They found Jez Yates down by the river this morning," she said suddenly. "Beaten almost to death, and an arm broken. They're talking about it along the street."

Oz shook his head.

"Who would do that to Jez? He's a good sort, gets on well enough with everyone. And him with the mill to run, and a young family."

Tammi coloured slightly, lowering her eyes.

"They're talking about my father," she said. "They stopped when they saw me coming, and watched me go by, but I heard them."

There was silence between the three of them for a long moment.

"He won't want you here," said Max at length, "talking to us."

"I know." She broke off for a moment. "I'll go home the long way, by the Sound. I just hoped you might know where she was."

"Have you looked up in the forest?" He hesitated. "She told me you knew where to go."

"Yes, I looked there first. Some of her things had gone, but she wasn't there." She looked at him again, glancing sidelong at Oz. "I'm always careful when I go up there, not to leave tracks."

Max nodded.

"I'm going to go fishing above the rapids this evening," Tammi said suddenly. "Maybe if either of us sees or hear anything, we could meet out there and tell each other."

"All right."

She smiled shyly at them.

"Thank you. I ought to go."

She slipped out of sight around the building, leaving Oz and Max looking at each other.

"You like to live dangerously," said Oz. "Now the other one."

"She's worried about her sister."

"And I'm worried about you." He shook his head. "I wonder what Jez Yates did to cross Taverner."

"I'll be careful, Oz."

"You'll only be careful when you stop having anything to do with those Taverner girls."

Max sighed.

"Let's have some food," he said. "Then do you want some help with those shoeing jobs that are coming in this afternoon?"

He worked all afternoon with Oz in the smithy, and then, the last horse shod, he went down to the river to wash himself and his clothes. It was warm and sheltered under the west facing crag by the washing pool, and deserted at this time of day; he took the rare opportunity to sun himself for a couple of hours as his clothes dried on a warm slab of rock. Now evening was drawing on, the sun dipping towards the peaks on the other side of the Sound, the air starting to cool. Mindful of his promise to Tammi, he stretched and put on his damp clothes. He walked slowly up the far bank in the evening sunlight, for once at peace with himself, lost in the sound of the river running between the rocks, watching the salmon leaping. He came to the place where he knew Trudie and her sister usually fished, but there was no one there. Frowning slightly, he walked slowly on, moving away from the river through a small alder grove to avoid some broken ground and another set of rapids. Coming back to the river where it ran fast and deep above the shallows, he saw them both on the opposite bank. He dropped silently to a knee there by the rocks, and watched.

Tammi was sitting on a rock with her back to the river, talking quietly to Trudie. Relief washed through him at the sight of Trudie, at the fact that she appeared unharmed. He watched her with her sister, the same slender frame, the same chaos of golden hair across the shoulders. He watched the way they held themselves, the closeness between them as they talked, the one in furs, the other in her village clothes. He listened to the sound of the river. Everything was all right, and there was no need now for him to intrude on their sisterhood. He turned, as silently as he had come, and walked slowly back beside the river. The light of the setting sun danced on the waves of the Sound, in perpetual movement, no two moments quite the same.

He crossed the river by the stone bridge just beyond the mill. Pausing for a long moment at the far end of the bridge, he turned towards the mill. He went softly up to the door, knocked, and waited.

After a time there was movement inside, and the door opened a little. The brown eyes of Orrie Yates, Jez's wife, regarded him suspiciously.

"I heard about Jez," Max said. "I came to say I'm sorry."

"Well you're the only one that has."

"How is he?"

She hesitated, then opened the door fully.

"You'd best come in and see for yourself." As he stepped in, at last able to see her properly, he could see the weariness and distress in her. "A visitor will take his mind off the state he's in."

Yates was sitting on his bed in their room at the end of the mill, his back to the wall, stripped to the waist. His arm had been roughly splinted, his face and body were a sea of bruises. One eye was black, the other almost closed with swelling. He was clearly still in considerable pain. Max entered quietly, Orrie behind him.

"You've got a visitor," she said.

Yates shifted, grimacing, looked up.

"Max."

"I heard this morning. I wondered how you were."

"I've been better." He winced, shifting again. "But I don't reckon there's anything that won't mend with time. Is it all over the village already then?"

"Tammi Taverner came by this morning, told us. Said she'd heard it in the street."

"I hope that's where she heard it." The miller took his wife's hand, looked up at her. "Would you leave me a few minutes with Max, Orrie dear? There's things I have to say to him I don't want you troubled with."

The door closed softly behind her, and Yates said:-

"What brought Tammi round the smithy?"

"She said she was looking for Trudie."

"And why the smithy?"

"She said she thought I might know."

"Yes." Yates looked at him thoughtfully.

Max sat down gently on the end of the bed.

"Was it Joss Taverner did this?"

"Him and Stu Bell." Yates grimaced painfully. "They owed me a few from the other night, but I hadn't reckoned on such a beating. Taverner's a vindictive bastard." He looked up at Max. "But never mind that. You say she was looking for Trudie."

"She said she'd disappeared. But it's all right now. I saw them both together just now, up the river."

"Thank God. I thought I might never see her alive again, when she took off into the night naked, while I was attending to that fat bastard Bell." He shook his head. "In her own bedroom, dear God." He hesitated for a moment, looking at Max. "You think a lot to her, don't you?"

Max nodded, looking down at the floor.

"We were in the ale house," Yates said. "Well, I do business with Taverner. Him, me, and Bell. We'd had a lot of ale, got talking about women, you know, the way you do. Bell said how well Trudie looked, and Taverner said, well, if that's what you think, she'll show you both a good time. Like I say, I was drunk, so I went along." He looked up at Max. "We were in her bedroom, the three of us, and she was looking up at us terrified, and then Taverner ripped everything off her. His own daughter, for God's sake. Suddenly it sickened me, us being there, the look on her face. All I could think of was my own little one asleep up here. Bell was on the bed, starting to touch her. I saw red. I laid Taverner out, he was drunk and wasn't expecting it, then I went for Bell. While we were at it she lit out of there, stark naked." He looked at Max again. "I've never seen a look quite like that in anyone's eyes."

"I have," Max answered softly. "In hers."

The miller nodded.

"I would have run, too," he said, "in her place."

Silence fell between them, then Max said:-

"She'll think that everyone knows now. She thinks like that."

Yates nodded.

"Bell didn't come out of it well enough to brag," he said. "Even though he's been back for his revenge since, now he's well enough."

"I'll tell her that. If I get the chance."

"You do that, Max." He closed his eyes painfully. "I'm grateful you looked in. I needed to get this whole sorry business off my chest to someone."

Max got to his feet.

"I'll look in again, Jez. Get Orrie to come round the smithy if there's anything needing doing."

He walked softly to the door, let himself out, murmured good-night to Orrie outside. As he stepped out into the night the sky was alive with stars, the great white banner of the Milky Way unfurled above his head. He waited at the end of the river bridge, listening to the water foaming over the rocks, until his eyes adapted to the dark. There was just enough light to see by, as he made his way home through the velvet night.

Five

The weather had closed in the night before, and today had dawned heavy and grey, with cloud low on the forest and the crag across the valley, and rain driving in off the Sound on a mild wind. Disinclined to venture out without good reason, Max had discovered that there was already pressure in the gas generator, and had started experimenting. He was able to work in the forge as Oz was between jobs, and in any event the smith's curiosity had got the better of him. At first impressed by the foot - long yellow flame issuing from the end of the pipe, he was now shaking his head.

"It's not a lot better than a candle flame. There's no heat to it."

Max stood with his arms folded, eyes narrowed, thinking.

"The charcoal doesn't burn hot unless you use the bellows. Anything needs air to burn." He hesitated. "What if we mixed air into the pipe?"

Fired by this new idea, he blew the flame out, bunged the end of the pipe. He spent the next half hour making a Y shaped union out of two offcuts of pipe, and connecting the bellows to one arm. Then he removed the bung, and, while Oz lit the gas again at the stem of the Y, he tensely welded the other arm onto the end of the pipe, hoping the heat would not ignite the gas inside.

"Try the bellows."

The smith started to pump, and at once the flame lengthened, turning to a light blue colour and making a roaring sound. Max directed it onto an iron on the forge. In what seemed moments, the iron was glowing cherry red. They grinned at each other in delight.

"We're on to something here."

"Damn - the pipe's melting."

They hastily stopped pumping, extinguished the gas, bunged the softened end of the pipe with difficulty. Max was frowning again.

"We need a better way of turning off the gas."

"Why not just make the end of the pipe out of metal for now?" Oz looked around the smithy. "We can use the end of that old set of bellows."

In a few more minutes Max had moulded the modified end of the gas pipe around the base of the old bellows nozzle, and the flame was on again. They found that they could control the temperature by varying the rate of pumping air, and that blowing too hard blew the flame out. Oz was grinning, shaking his head.

"You have some good ideas, Max, I'll give you that," he said. "I did have doubts about this one, with all the trouble and mess it's caused, but I reckon I've got to hand it to you."

Max was rubbing his cheek, thinking again.

"The details need sorting out," he said. "We need a way of turning the gas on and off, and a way of stopping the generator lining bursting if the gas builds up. I hadn't really thought all that through." Abruptly, he broke off, stood immobile, with a troubled, intent expression on his face.

Oz frowned.

"What's the -"

Max was on his way to the door.

"Trudie," he cast back over his shoulder. "Something's wrong."

He was gone, into the rain, leaving the door swinging behind him. By the time the smith had reached the door, looked up the street, Max had vanished from sight between the houses. Shaking his head, he went slowly back inside.

Max hesitated at the end of the village street. Already, he was wet through with the rain, his hair plastered to his forehead. The feeling in his head was a little like a bright light and a loud noise in the back of his skull. All his senses still worked, but it overwhelmed all his thoughts, its urgency filling his mind. He knew that it was Trudie, in the way he would have known her voice, or the sight or scent of her, and he knew that she was terrified. Terrified and alone, and that she expected to die. He knew that it was coming from up the valley. He started to run up the track, his back to the rain, towards the cloud shrouded forest, cursing his stunted legs, the muscles in them starting to burn as he climbed. Soon he was among the trees, and then in the cloud, in the vast gloomy spaces of the forest, one tree misting into the next, the rain running down his face and into his eyes. He moved without any of his normal caution, driving himself on, his legs and his chest on fire, his mind full of her terror.

In a few minutes he came to the crag by the waterfall. The rocks glistened with water. At first he climbed wildly, then his foot slipped, and he was left for a moment hanging from his fingertips, both feet scrabbling for a hold. After that he forced himself to stand still against the rock, take a few seconds' worth of deep, gasping breaths. Then he climbed on, more steadily and carefully now, testing each hold for grip and security. Still she burned in his mind. The fear was palpable, as if it was his own. He scrambled to the top of the crag, stood beside the river where it unwound into space.

The valley ran away into the cloud, the trees like grey ghosts, like skeletons, only half real in the mist. She was up there somewhere, perhaps even at her shelter. Impulsively, he forded the river above the next pool, almost falling, one foot going into the icy water. He headed up the far bank at a stumbling run, scrambling over the outcrops of rock. In his mind the fear went on, driving him on, but better, better by far than his own fear, the fear that the feeling in his head would stop, meaning her death. He could not conceive of what her death would mean. He ran on, wiping rain and sweat from his eyes.

Rounding an outcrop as he climbed, he came suddenly on a wolf. It lay lifeless on a patch of grass, two arrows in its neck. Another of the strange wolves, its body still warm, the blood still wet on it. Dully, knowing what he would find, he pulled the arrows from it. The arrow heads were copper, the ones he and Oz had made. Instinctively, his hand went to his shoulder, and at once fear and dismay washed through him. In his haste and preoccupation, he had forgotten his bow.

Slowly, he put the arrows in his belt. It made no difference. Rousing himself, he forced his legs to move once again, until he saw the silhouette of the rocky spur on the valley wall which shielded her cave. He paused for a moment, his thoughts racing. After a moment he began to climb the back of the spur. In his mind, her knowledge of her coming death still burned.

He climbed fast, his mind like a mirror now, intent, concentration fixed on the climbing, on moving almost noiselessly over the rock. When he judged he was some twenty feet above the level of the cave, he began carefully traversing the face of the crag, until he could see round it, up the valley. His body like a coiled spring, he checked each hold for loose debris, whose fall might give him away. Suddenly, he could see down onto the opening of the cave.

She was standing in its mouth, he saw, soaked to the skin by the rain, her shelter half wrecked. Facing her, little over an arm's length away, was another of the wolves. She was protected by the narrow cave mouth, and it could only approach her from the front. She had plainly run out of arrows. The wolf made little lunges at her, and she was keeping it at bay with the end of her bow, using it as he had used his in the high woods. He could see that she was exhausted, after what must have been at least half an hour, and that she moved the bow more slowly, so that the wolf came closer to taking it in its jaws. His hand strayed to the small knife at his belt.

Noiselessly, he began descending the spur, keeping to one side of the cave, heading for a bluff on its nearer side. Quietly, desperately, Trudie fought for her life below him, as he tried to concentrate on the rock. As his feet found the bluff, he heard the clatter of wood, heard her give a little sob. Her wash of fear exploded in his mind like a wave, momentarily blanking out the world. Looking down, he saw that the wolf had got the bow in its jaws, had wrested it from her grasp. In panic, she grabbed at a broken pole from her shelter, held that before her instead. The animal stood immobile again, watching her.

Poised atop the bluff, he tried to shut it all out. He tensed his legs, wiping his hands on his sodden trousers, and took the little knife in both hands. He looked down on the wolf's grey back fifteen feet or so below, knowing he would have only one chance, fixating his vision on the place where the neck met the skull. He tightened his grip on the knife, and jumped. For a frozen moment he seemed to hang in the air.

He landed half across the wolf, carrying it to the ground, driving the knife's full blade length into the place he had intended. He heard something crack, the breath was driven out of him, there was a blaze of pain as his knee struck the rocky ground. The wolf jerked convulsively beneath him, moved again, and was still. Gasping for breath, he rolled off the wolf, doubled up, his face against the sodden grey fur. It was done.

So slowly, the world came back. The smell of wet dog in his nose, the rain on his back. Suddenly he felt icy cold. He could not stop himself from shaking. Painfully, he sat up, his injured knee crying out in protest.

Trudie was leaning against the rock in the cave mouth, the stick lying at her feet. In her eyes was the blankness of shock. He could see her shaking from where he lay. He tried to put weight on his knee, found he could not. Abruptly, she sat down against the rock and started crying, the sobs racking her body. He dragged himself, at a half crawl, across the ground to where she lay. He put his arm round her, as she cried, hopelessly, her sodden hair across her back. They sat against the rock for a long time, as the tension slowly left them.

At last she lifted her head, rubbing her eyes, with a look that would burn in his memory for the rest of his life. Again that incredible wave of empathy broke between them, leaving them both without any need for words, and she flung her arms around his shoulders, crying again.

"Max, Max," she whispered, her head against his shoulder. "I don't understand."

"You don't need to understand."

"You knew." She unclasped her arms, holding both his shoulders so she could look into his face. "Somehow you knew." Her eyes narrowed a little, in wonder. "Again."

He nodded slowly, as uncertain as she, and she lowered her hands.

"I felt you in my head," he said, his eyes clouded, looking away. "I felt your fear. I knew you were going to die." He looked back at her. "I couldn't do anything but run. I didn't even think of my bow."

Again, tears filled her eyes.

"Why am I worth so much to you?" she asked. "I don't understand."

"Don't you know?"

"You take such terrible risks. Twice, now, you've put your life between me and my death."

"We've both suffered," he said. "You learn the value of things. I would do anything to keep you from harm."

She looked at him, a peculiar luminosity in her gaze, yet, behind it, the fear of closeness, the hesitation, the wanting to run.

"The way you are helps me go on."

"And you, me." He looked away, his eyes momentarily unfocussed. "I thought I would lose you, today."

"Oh, Max." She shook her head. "I don't know. I don't know about anything any more."

"I know that you're everything to me."

She looked desperately sad, gazing out between the mist shrouded trees.

"All I know how to do is hide from people, make myself small, fight for my life when there's no other way. I can look after myself, because I don't really matter, but not anyone else."

"I don't care. It's the way you are that I would die for." He rested his hand on hers, wet with the rain, one as cold as the other. "But I think you know that. Trudie, what's going on?"

She looked up at him.

"I don't know," she said. "I told you I can go out in the forest in my mind. When we met the first wolf together, I learned that it's real. But I didn't do anything, today. Except that I knew that the second wolf would kill me."

"You were in my head," he said. "You, as if I could reach out and touch you. You never have been before, not like that. I don't understand."

"Perhaps you're like me," she said slowly, wonderingly. "You're good in the forest, nothing ever surprises you." Again, the luminous look came into her eyes. "Sometimes you know how I feel. And you're here."

"But I can't do any of these things you say you can."

"No." The look in her eyes faded, and she looked away. "I told you I don't know. But you're here."

"Yes." He shivered.

"There's something else," she said. "I told you in the Ruins, I know if I'm being followed. But these wolves are different. I never know they're there. That's why I was surprised and nearly killed, today."

They sat beside each other in silence for a long time, then he noticed she was shivering too.

"You're frozen."

"So are you." She got painfully to her feet, stretching stiff legs. "I've got some dry things in the cave, for you as well as me. Come out of the rain."

When he tried to move, he found he could put no weight on the injured knee. Pulling up his trouser leg to examine it, he saw a deep gash, and the whole joint swollen, beginning to turn dark with bruising. She had come back to him, was bending over him, gently touching it.

"Look what you've done."

"I expect it'll be all right. But I can't stand on it."

"I've got arnica," she said. "I'll strap it up. But we must get you out of the rain."

She put his arm around her shoulders, and struggled to her feet with him. Despite his size, he was strong, and heavier than she had expected. She helped him inside the cave, sat him down again on a mat of dry grass. She took some cloth off a rock shelf, and tore it into strips.

"I need to go for water," she said.

"Take your bow," he said. "And the two arrows I was carrying."

"The bow needs a new string. And the arrows were both broken when you fell," she called back from outside the cave. "I'll be careful." And she was gone, into the cloud, leaving him in the cold silence of the cave. He was not normally prey to fear, but was still glad when she returned, a few minutes later, with some river water in a pot. She stood, hands on hips, regarding him with a mischievous smile.

"Choose," she said. "Girl's clothes or furs."

He grinned despite himself.

"Furs, I suppose."

"Take your clothes off. Then I'll bandage it up."

He hesitated, then struggled to do so, and she helped him, giggling at his pathetic attempts at modesty, only making matters worse. She helped him into the furs, wrapped another around his shoulders, and he felt warmth slowly beginning to return. She made a paste with the river water, the arnica, and some other herbs from her collection, strapped it to the cut and bruised areas of his knee, and bound it up firmly with wet and then dry strips of cloth, to support the knee. He watched her as she bent over his leg, her hair falling down as she worked. He could hear her teeth chattering, her skin was blue with cold.

"Leave it, Trudie," he said. "You must get warm."

"It's done," she said, straightening up. She took some clothes from a rock ledge further inside the cave, and then, without inhibition, let the waterlogged furs fall to the floor at her feet. He looked at her, the body without an ounce of excess weight, the finely muscled legs and arms, the small, near adolescent breasts, the intersecting ruin of scars across her back.

"You're beautiful," he said wonderingly, as if surprised at himself.

She stopped, looked at him.

"I'm too tall, too skinny, and my back's a mess."

"I know what I see. And you know what I see, too." His eyes met hers. "If you want to."

"I've never tried to look. Wouldn't. Unless . . . unless, maybe, you told me to."

He held her gaze.

"Go on, then."

She hesitated.

"All right. If you're sure." She finished dressing, then paused for a moment, closing her eyes, composing her face as if withdrawing from the material world. Abruptly, incredibly, he sensed her in his head, like the cool touch of a beautiful woman turning pages, gently inspecting his thoughts. She must have felt him start, because her eyes opened, full of concern.

"I'm sorry -"

"No, no. It's all right. Stay." He marshalled his thoughts. "Here. Here's what I wanted you to see."

He remembered her then, working beside him in the Ruins, launching the boat, walking under trees in sunlight. Confronting a wolf that was about to kill him, with only a stone in her bare hands. The way she walked, the way the wind played with her hair, the sunlight on her skin, the way her muscles rippled when she moved. The sun in her eyes like fathomless water. He let the emotions well up, how he felt when he saw these things, how she filled the world for him, seemed to embody all he had ever lived for. The way he felt when she looked at him that time in the barn, just now, after he had killed the wolf, the aching quality her beauty had for him. He had no words for these things, but the sense of them filled his mind. And he knew that she saw it. He felt her take his hand, squeeze it painfully, and, opening his eyes, he saw tears standing in hers.

"There," he said. "That's what I wanted to show you."

"That isn't me."

He smiled sadly.

"I'm the one on the outside. I know what I see. You know I've seen all the other stuff too. It only makes you more beautiful."

Tears filled her eyes again.

"Thank you for not running, not despising. For not thinking I'm filthy."

"You know, now, what I think."

She held his gaze, sniffing, wiping her eyes.

"Never again, Max," she said. "I promise. Unless you tell me to."

"I know I can trust you."

They fell silent for a few moments, then she asked:-

"What am I, Max? What is this seeing?"

"I don't know." He sighed, remembering the look of puzzled surprise on Oz's face as he left the smithy. "I think it's totally new." He looked up at her. "No maps."

"No maps." She hesitated, looking down at the ground. "For years I thought I was alone, that no one would ever know. I knew I was different. It's made me a little strange." She met his gaze. "But you know, now."

He nodded, thoughtfully.

"Have you been able to do it for years?"

"Some of it. But I've learned so much more these last few months."

"I can meet you, like just now," he said. "But I can't do the animal stuff. The out in the forest stuff."

"You're good in the forest."

"I don't know I'm being followed, like you. I just have a sort of sixth sense." He paused. "What about Tammi?"

"I think maybe she's like you. I'm not really sure. I don't think she goes where I do. We've never talked about it."

"Then there's these wolves," he said after a moment. "No one else has ever seen them."

"No."

"And you aren't aware of them." His eyes were almost black in the gloom of the cave mouth. "I wonder if they're aware of you. I wonder if you draw them somehow. If they've got something of what you've got. Maybe they can shut you out."

She paled.

"I hadn't thought of that. I never looked. Both times I've been too terrified."

"You won't be safe alone here, now."

She looked down at the floor of the cave.

"I know." She shook her head, hopelessly. "But I can't go back."

"You *have* to," he said. "For now. Even though I know what it costs. It's still better than that." He pointed at the body of the wolf. "Come back, at least until we work out what to do."

Trudie was silent for a moment. At length she shook her head.

"There isn't any choice, is there?" She paused, frowning. "Though there is one thing I'm going to try."

"What's that?"

"I'll tell you if it works." She got to her feet. "Let me help you. We have to see if you can walk."

He could not, unaided, but found he could if he put an arm around her shoulder and leaned on a stick from her wrecked shelter. The journey back would be difficult, but not impossible. She re-strung her bow, running her fingers thoughtfully over the teeth marks in the wood, and then went outside and dragged the wolf's body some way down the slope. The rain had thinned to a light drizzle, but cloud still blanketed the valley.

Max balled up his wet clothes, and spent a few minutes binding up the breaks in the arrows he had taken from the wolf with some twine she had. She put them in her empty quiver. These and their two knives were the only weapons they had. Then, painfully slowly, they set off down the valley, she bent down to his height, the bow and quiver on her back.

It did not take them many minutes to realise that Max would be unable to cross the river. It took all the rest of the day to make their way down the far bank to the cultivated land, the detour round the rough ground by the waterfall taking hours, with dusk thickening under a heavy sky. It was fully dark by the time they came down to the bridge by the mill.

"You can't take me into the village," he said as they crossed the bridge. "We're bound to be seen, and you know what'll happen."

"I'm not going to leave you."

"I'll go to the mill. Orrie will take me in. I can dry my clothes there too, and come on in the morning, in my own clothes. I'll think of a story about the knee. That way you can slip back to the farm tonight, with no one about."

She hesitated, seeing the sense in it.

"Go on," he said. "I'll be all right."

She took both his hands in hers, turned to face him.

"No one's ever looked at me the way you did today."

"Go on," he said again. "And be careful."

Without another word she turned away, down the path to the village. He watched the night swallow her, then he turned towards the mill. He had underestimated the pain and difficulty involved in walking, and it took him twenty more minutes to get to the door, climb the steps until he could knock.

The miller was back on his feet, though still badly bruised, and if he and his wife were surprised at Max appearing on their threshold after dark, disabled and clad in furs, they concealed it well. His exhaustion must have been apparent, because they helped him to the couch in the corner without many words being spoken. Within a few minutes he had fallen into deep, dreamless sleep.

Six

Max had woken late the next morning, his mind momentarily blank on finding himself on the couch in the corner of the mill cottage, then memory had come flooding back. He had spent some time talking to Jez, who, being unable to work, had been looking for conversation. He told him the outline of the previous day's events, glossing over the parts that would be hard to believe, that he sensed would be better kept quiet anyway. Orrie had insisted on feeding him, on looking at his knee. The arnica had worked its usual magic on the bruising, and though the joint was still very painful, he found it easier already to put weight on it, to bend it slightly. It was late morning when, leaning on a crutch that he and Jez had improvised between them, he thanked his hosts for their kindness to him, laughing at the idea that he had been offering them help only a couple of days earlier. Dressed again in his own clothes, he set off down the track to the village, in a fitful sunny interval between broken cloud. In contrast to yesterday, he found he could cover ground reasonably quickly with the aid of the crutch. He attracted a few incurious stares as he came into the village, and soon he was leaning on the door frame of the smithy, greeting Oz.

"The warrior returns." The smith looked at him with evident relief. "I wondered if I'd be seeing you again, taking off into the forest like that without your bow. You're a bloody fool, Max."

"I won't be doing it again. I couldn't think straight yesterday."

"Was it Trudie?"

He nodded.

"Up above the falls. She'd killed a wolf, run out of arrows, and its mate had her cornered in a cave."

"Bloody hell." He shook his head slowly. "And you without a bow. What did you do?"

He grinned sheepishly.

"Jumped it. Got it with my knife."

"You need your bloody head examined."

"Probably. But it'd have had her otherwise."

"And that's how you did your leg?"

"It's mending already. She strapped it up for me."

"I'm sure she did, after all that."

He grinned.

"Lay off, Oz. You're meant to be showing concern, not winding me up."

Oz put down the hammer he had been holding.

"Come and sit down," he said, suddenly serious. "You can tell me all about it, and I've things to tell you too. But first, I've something to show you. I've been making a bit for your new toy while you were off playing the hero. Remember you said you needed a way of turning your gas off?"

Max turned the beautifully cast copper tap over in his hands, looking at the perfectly ground taper, the iron spring, down the stub pipes to see how it worked.

"Nice, Oz" he said simply. "Really nice. One out of two problems solved." He smiled. "I've still got two good arms. We can fit it this afternoon."

"If what I've got to tell you doesn't take your mind off it. But come and have a bite to eat first."

Oz got out bread, cheese, and a jug of ale, and they sat down at the table, facing each other.

"Tell me something," the smith asked. "How did you know she was in trouble?"

Max met his eyes.

"If I can trust anyone, I can trust you, Oz," he said. "I can kind of hear her sometimes. Inside my head."

"Don't take the piss."

"Explain it, then. Any other way. If you can."

The grey eyes watched him for a long time. At length Max said:-

"Sometimes each of us knows what the other's thinking. I'm not talking about guesswork, intuition. I'm talking about knowing. She's far better at it than me. She knows what's moving around her, in the forest. And she can call. Like yesterday. But she didn't know what she was doing." His finger played with the breadcrumbs on the table.

They were both silent for a long time. At last Oz said:-

"I've never heard of anything like this."

"I'd never heard of wolves the size of donkeys."

"Now you are winding me up."

"I could show you a body," he said wearily. "But I'd think twice before going up the valley, now. I used to feel safe in the forest, if I kept my wits about me." He smiled ironically. "If I remembered my bow."

The smith was shaking his head.

"Where's all this coming from?"

"Who knows? People say poison from before makes people barren, causes freaks like me. Trudie said she'd seen plants, animals, even people down the Sound who don't look right. What if something wasn't right, but it worked?"

"Like you?"

He grinned, despite himself.

"Maybe." He fell silent for a while, then he said:-

"You said you had stuff to tell me."

"Yes." Oz looked at him, his eyes suddenly bleak. "I met Jez Yates in the village yesterday. He told me a few things. Said he'd told you, and wanted me to know the score too. So I'd know where you were coming from."

Max was looking down at the table again.

"Jez is all right," he said.

Oz was still looking at him.

"Mik Lundgren came by this morning," he said. "After more of your fish hooks. He'd been chatting in the village. Seems there were terrible screams coming from the Taverner place last night." He sighed. "A woman's screams. Quite early on. They were all talking about it."

Max was aware of the grain of the table's wood in astonishing detail.

"Right," he said.

"But you were with her."

"Depends when." Max's eyes narrowed. "I've never known her scream. She's got more guts in her little finger than I have in my whole body." He hesitated. "So who else could it have been?"

Wordlessly, their eyes met. When Oz spoke, it was with a venom that Max had never heard before.

"God, he's an evil bastard."

Max reached for his crutch, got slowly to his feet.

"I'm going round there," he said.

"Don't be a bloody fool. You know what he's like."

"No, don't *you* be a bloody fool." His voice was shaking with anger. "You heard the stuff I've told you. I'm sick of pretending this shit doesn't happen."

"Then take your bow."

"I'll kill him if I do." He made for the door.

Oz got to his feet.

"I'll give you five minutes," he said wearily. "Then I'll come in after you."

Later, Max remembered nothing of the walk through the village to the farm, though it must have taken him over five minutes with the crutch, though he must have passed people he would normally have greeted. The oak and nails of the Taverner door were in front of his face. He thumped on it with the crutch, his mind empty of everything. Perhaps the man was out on the farm, but he had seen no one in the fields.

There was movement in the house. Abruptly, the door opened, and Taverner stood there, his bulk filling the door frame. He had clearly been drinking.

"Well, if it isn't the dwarf," he said. "And what can I do for you?"

"I've come to see Trudie."

Taverner's eyes narrowed.

"I thought I'd told you what I'd do if you kept hanging around her," he said. "And you come to the front door in broad daylight."

"Yes, you told me."

"Then you'd best come in, I suppose." He turned away from the door, and Max followed him down the passage to the kitchen, leaving the door open. Suddenly, as Max came into the room, Taverner whirled on him, kicking the crutch away.

"Look at you," he said derisively. "Not even a man. What do you want with her? D'you fancy her yourself, is that it?"

Max steadied himself on a chair back.

"I just want to talk to her."

"What you want doesn't signify." He pushed Max hard in the chest, and he staggered, still holding on to the chair.

"I want to see her," he repeated.

"Well you can't."

Max's face hardened.

"I want to see them both. See if they're all right. Half the village heard the screaming last night."

"They did, did they? And that should worry me?"

"I know what you do with her," Max said. "I know who was screaming last night."

"You do, do you? You're smart for a freak."

"Got them locked up somewhere, have you? Your own daughters, like farm animals?"

Abruptly, Taverner swung at Max. He ducked, still holding the chair, and the punch missed. The farmer staggered, clearly drunker than he seemed.

"Got them chained to the bed, so they're ready for you? So they can't run, however much you disgust them?"

Enraged, Taverner turned on him again. Releasing the chair, Max staggered towards the corner of the room, where his crutch had fallen. As he got to it Taverner was on him, kicking him in the back of his injured knee. He fell on the crutch in a blaze of pain, his fingers closing on it as a second kick landed on his side, driving the wind from his body. He rolled, trying to bring the crutch down across the man's leg, but he had insufficient room to swing it, and Taverner was too heavy to unbalance. The crutch was wrenched from his grasp, flung aside. Gasping for breath, oblivious of the pain in his knee, Max dragged himself crab like across the floor, under the kitchen table. Taverner kicked a chair out of the way, then flung the table on its side, the crockery on it exploding across the flagstones. Max grabbed a chair, held it in front of him. Abruptly, Taverner looked up, his attention distracted. Oz, carrying an iron in one hand and a hand axe in the other, had appeared in the doorway.

"Come on, then," he said softly.

Suddenly Max threw the chair he was holding at Taverner. The man caught it easily, dashed it on the ground, bent and took up a leg in each hand. He backed into a corner, stood watching them with narrowed eyes, poised.

Again, Max scrabbled across the floor, had his crutch in his hand again. He swung it with all his strength at ground level, using both arms this time. It struck Taverner on the ankle, momentarily unbalancing him, as the man swung wildly with the chair leg, catching Max a blinding blow on the cheekbone. As Taverner brought his arm up, Oz was on him, bringing the iron down with all his strength on the arm. Taverner grunted in pain, dropped one of the chair legs, as Oz sliced with the axe in his other hand, opening a deep gash across the farmer's upper leg. The man hesitated for a moment, looked down at his leg in unbelief, as blood burst from the wound, and Oz swung back with the axe reversed, hitting him on the shoulder, catching him off balance. Max swung at his ankles again with the crutch, and he went down heavily, striking his head hard on the flagstones. He moaned once, and lay still, the blood welling from his leg, starting to pool on the floor.

"Filthy bastard." Oz was breathing heavily. "We ought to finish him off." He turned to Max. "Are you all right?"

Max nodded, slightly dazed.

"He's buggered my knee again, but yes, I think so." He looked up at the smith. "Thanks, Oz. He might have killed me."

"Might well have." Oz sighed. "Can't leave the bastard to bleed to death, I suppose. They'll only come after us."

He tore some strips from the tablecloth where it lay on the floor, tied them roughly around the wound on Taverner's leg. Satisfied that he had almost stopped the bleeding, he turned back to Max.

"Are you sure you're all right?"

Max nodded.

"Right." Oz straightened, picking up his axe and iron. "I'll search the house and barns for the girls."

Max grimaced.

"I'll wait here."

He heard Oz moving about the house, one door upstairs splintering open. He came downstairs again, shaking his head, and went outside into the farmyard. Max had recovered the crutch, and had got painfully to his feet by the time the smith returned.

"She's not here. Nor her sister."

"She'll have taken her into the forest. It's what she does, when she can't stand things any more." Max shook his head hopelessly. "But we'd decided it was too dangerous, with the wolves."

Oz looked at him.

"I don't suppose there's much you or I can do about that now."

Max shook his head slowly.

"No."

On the floor, Taverner groaned. Oz bent across him, spat in his face.

"Don't even think of coming round the smithy," he said. "We'll be looking out for you, and we'll maim you next time." He straightened up, took Max's arm around his own shoulders. "Come on, Max. Leave him there. If that wound opens, bugger it, no one can say we didn't try."

Outside, the light was blinding after the gloom of the house. They walked slowly back through the village, one leaning on the other.

Impatience and frustration dominated the next few days for Max, while he waited for his knee to heal. Oz had got him more healing herbs from old Sue Pritchard in the village, and quite soon he could walk without the crutch, though he would need a stick for a few days yet. He did not yet dare to trust the knee over any distance, especially on a climb or on broken ground. He knew in his heart that it would have been stupid to risk permanent damage to the joint, or death at the jaws of a wolf, for the sake of a few days, however high the stakes. He wanted desperately to talk to Trudie, would have settled for a glimpse of her in the distance, but he knew that there was nothing to be done. He thought of asking Oz to go up to the cave shelter, but was unwilling to reveal its location to him, unwilling to expose him to wolf attack in the forest. He knew, too, that it was even possible that the girls would try to kill Oz if he went to the shelter alone, distraught as they doubtless were. He knew that he had no way of knowing if they had even gone to the shelter. He could do nothing but hope that the absence of Trudie from his mind meant that they were alive and safe. He wondered that he had not known what she had found when she returned to the farm, and then realised that he had probably already been in exhausted sleep by then, down at the mill.

Concern for her filled his waking hours, and he went over and over, in his mind, the events of the past couple of weeks, seeing no reason to change his interpretation of them. He made the waiting more bearable by fitting the gas valve Oz had made, and designing a pressure release device for the generator based on a head of water, though he was not yet mobile enough to build it. Then he remembered the building in the Ruins, remembered seeing wider pipe there which would be ideally suited to this purpose. He decided to sail down next day. He would take his usual weapons, and his knee could continue to mend in the boat. He might find other useful items while he was about it. Deeply, shamefully, he also knew that he wanted to be miles away from a call from Trudie which he had no ability to answer, to be forced to sit there, waiting for it to end.

Oz was visibly unhappy at the idea of his going down the Sound in anything less than perfect health, but he could see that Max was unable to settle to anything, and accepted that the knee would continue to heal in the boat. Grudgingly, he finally dropped his objections, checking Max's equipment with him in a way he never had before. He even came down to the jetty an hour or so after dawn, to help him load and launch the boat, and to check that he could manage the sails.

Max felt better once he was out on the water, watching the sunlight splintering on the wavetops, the forested shore glide past. As the village fell away astern, he breathed more easily, began to realise how heavily the events of the previous days had been weighing on his mind. He remembered Taverner bleeding on his kitchen floor, the smell of wolf in his nose, and Trudie asking him what she was. He remembered her saying how the wolves could surprise her, as he stared sightlessly into the water, as it moved against the boat.

A brisk southerly breeze was blowing up the Sound from the direction of the Ruins. He left his improvised steering gear disconnected, sailing the boat himself all day, zigzagging across the wind. Pleased at the way getting the best out of the boat occupied his mind, at getting only the occasional twinge from his knee, he was surprised to see how much the day had drawn on. A little before sunset, he moored in the lee of a small rocky island a few hundred yards offshore, and ate some food; then, as the breeze dropped and the dusk thickened, he covered himself with a sail, settled down in the boat to sleep.

Next morning dawned bright and cloudless, and he was soon out on the Sound again, with the breeze in the same quarter as before. He frowned at the shore, thinking about timing. At this rate of progress he should be at the Ruins around dusk. He decided to spend the night in the same flooded building as on his previous visit, landing at dawn the following morning. His attention divided between his thoughts and sailing the boat, the day passed much as the one before. He rounded the point to the bay of the Ruins as the sun touched the peaks across the Sound, with barely enough breeze to carry him inshore to his mooring, as night stole over the water, the colours of sunset fading into the dusk. The Ruins seemed as deserted as they always were. Preoccupied with the boat, and his own thoughts, he made fast, ate some berries he had brought. By then it was dark, and he lay down in the boat and slept.

Refreshed, he awoke well after dawn. After a little breakfast, he rowed the boat over to the street end where he normally landed. Pulling the boat up on the shore, he went round the corner to where he normally left his cart.

It was not there.

His mind raced. He was momentarily paralysed by the unexpectedness of it, after the predictability of the previous visits. His first thought was ambush, but the ruined walls and windows seemed deserted. Unshouldering his bow, nocking an arrow, he searched the immediate area with great caution, cursing himself for becoming careless. Thoughtfully, he went back to the boat, got into it, moved it round to the hiding place he had used when he thought he was observed on the previous visit. He prepared his pack for a day's work, climbed over the wall, dropped onto the street, thankful at feeling only the mildest discomfort from his knee.

He hesitated by the wall, the Sound at his back. This put a different complexion on things. He could still try to get what he had come for, but the second day of leisurely exploration which he had half planned might now be foolhardy. Simply trying to get what he had come for might turn out to be foolhardy, with no cart, a knee that was still healing, and no prospect of assistance from anyone else. The two quivers of arrows on his back were reassuring.

Still he hesitated. Everything depended on who had taken the cart. Some lone traveller might have thought it useful to take into the Ruins, it might even, remotely possibly, have been taken by Trudie and Tammi, though he was certain Trudie was far away in the forest, would not risk Tammi's life by bringing her here. But if it had been taken by the people Trudie had said lived here, further into the Ruins, who were presumably here in some numbers, they might have drawn conclusions from the cart's presence, and the other signs he had no doubt left here and there. If they had taken it, then they might be watching him now. He hesitated, thinking how dependent his future plans had become on continued access to this place's resources, at least until the events of recent weeks. At last he sighed, and keeping his bow at the ready, walked cautiously away from the water, keeping close to the wall. He would at least try to get what he had come for, for better or for worse, and there was a slender chance that he might recover the cart.

He moved slowly up the street, keeping close to walls, carefully checking every corner and doorway so far as he could, passing quickly across openings to buildings, never leaving his back to them. He deviated in places from his normal route, though this, too, cost him extra time. It took him fully half an hour to get to the large building he had visited previously, and in that time he saw nothing untoward, not even a single animal.

He went down the ramp, into the building with all his usual caution, spending many minutes searching the aisles for anything that might be there. Eventually he relaxed a little, remembering where he had seen the straight lengths of larger pipe, about the diameter of his thigh. He was removing the first, wincing at the noise it made, when he caught movement out of the corner of his eye.

Seven

Max whirled, just in time to see something melt into invisibility behind the racks. Dropping the pipe, oblivious of the noise he made, he ran along the aisle to the next corner, crouched there immobile, heart pounding, ears straining for the slightest sound. Silence. Then he heard the faintest movement, back from the direction he had come. He readied his bow, then suddenly fear cramped his guts. Movement again, but off to his right. He was too exposed here. He looked over his shoulder, hesitated momentarily, then turned and ran down the aisle, jinking as he went, away from the ramp. He could feel his knee protesting.

Where the aisle ended, perhaps a couple of hundred feet away, there was a doorway in the wall. He sprinted for it. As he dived into the doorway an arrow swished past his shoulder, bounced off the wall, clattered onto the floor at his feet. People, more than one of them, and unfriendly. Perhaps, this time, he had taken a step too far. The arrow had a metal head, he saw, nicely made, in an alloy unfamiliar to him. These people were serious.

He leaned against the wall, breathing heavily, his heart racing. Behind him, a staircase led upwards, He listened, could hear nothing. Darting a glance round the door frame elicited another arrow, singing out of the gloom, clattering harmlessly off the wall behind him. Clearly he had no chance here, as there were evidently at least two of them. He turned and ran up the staircase, cursing the footprints he left in the dust, hoping they were a little way behind him. As he ran, he remembered with a chill that the building's two top storeys had collapsed. Around a corner, and the stairwell was completely blocked with rubble. They had him trapped. He turned, his mind working furiously, then ran back down, cat-like, to the turn in the stairs, pressing his back against the wall. He waited silently, listening, an arrow between his teeth and another nocked in the bow. He could hear his heartbeat, his hands were moist where they held the bow. It was very dark in the stairwell.

Suddenly there was a sound on the stairs. Now. He leaped out from behind the wall with bow drawn, shouting at the top of his voice, letting his arrow fly at the first of the two figures on the stairs, silhouetted in the dim light coming from below. It took the man full in the chest, and he went back on the one behind him, his own arrow clattering off the ceiling. Max rushed down on them, the other arrow in his bow now, releasing it into the ribs of the second struggling figure at the bottom of the stairs as he passed. He shivered, remembering what Trudie had said, as he burst from the doorway, grabbing another arrow from his quiver, sprinting along the wall. Maybe there were only two of them. Or if there were more, maybe the others were further back. He jinked, ran into an aisle, stopping after a moment or two to listen intently. Nothing. Then abruptly an arrow ricocheted off the metal support close to his head, striking a spark. But it had come from behind. Once again he sprinted, darting through from one aisle to another, heading now for the ramp. One more arrow whistled past him, but no one was visible.

"He's coming out!"

The shout from behind him was guttural, the intonation unfamiliar, but the meaning was perfectly clear, the language a variant of his own. So there were more of them outside. The ones inside would cut him off if he tried for the other ramp, and he could feel his knee protesting. Better to die in sunlight. He sprinted for the ramp entrance, burst into the light. There were two of them there, both women, one holding a bow. He stopped to aim as she raised it, his own arrow lancing into her shoulder as she fired, throwing her off balance. She screamed, as he swung his bow at the other woman, dodging round her up the ramp. Reaching the street, he snatched a glance over his shoulder, saw, to his relief, that she was bending over the other, crouched on the ground.

He turned to his right, towards the Sound, and had run down as far as the next building when he thought he saw movement in a window opening across the street. Next moment pain whiplashed through his calf. He looked down, stupefied, to see an arrow embedded in it, which had passed right through the muscle. The pain searing through him, he half staggered, half ran towards the small building on his right, a second arrow narrowly missing him as he went. Teeth gritted, he turned in the doorway of the building. The other had made the mistake of breaking cover, and was sprinting towards him. Max's arrow took him in the chest, and he fell, rolled over twice, and lay still. Suddenly it was very quiet.

Max looked up the street, saw people emerging from the building in which he had been discovered. There were at least five of them. Grimacing, trying to hold the arrow shaft still, trying not to cry out with the pain, he snapped the shaft near the head, and jerked the rest of it out of his leg. There was some blood, but, incredibly, it seemed to have missed any major vessels. He bound his scarf tightly round the wounds, turned back to inspect the building. Running was clearly out of the question now. He needed to find somewhere where he could not be surprised from behind, where there was some chance of holding them off, at least until he ran out of arrows. No point in trying to hide, with the body outside in the street.

The door ahead of him opened into a staircase, made of the same white material as the larger building, running up. He climbed painfully to the first floor. The room facing the stairwell looked out over the street, commanded the top of the stair. It would have to do. He took off his pack and one quiver, laid them at his feet. He had twelve arrows left. Very slowly, he moved to look out through the window opening, watch them coming down the street, joined by two more who came cautiously out of the building across the road, pointing at their fallen comrade, at the building in which he now was. Seven of them, four of them women, each with bows and plenty of arrows. What the hell. He got to his feet, loosed an arrow, and one of the women screamed and went down. The others scattered in all directions, three of them disappearing below him, presumably entering the building. He squatted down, his back against the wall, and nocked another arrow, waiting.

After a moment there was a noise on the stairs, and he drew his bow. A head appeared above the top step, dark eyes regarding him for a frozen moment, as he loosed the arrow, taking the man in the cheek. He screamed horribly, toppling back down the stairs. Max shivered, nocking another arrow. At the bottom of the stairs the noise went on, dying away into inaudibility as the minutes passed. He listened as the silence returned.

After a long time he got cautiously to his feet, trying to see out of the window. At once there was a shout outside, and an arrow missed his head by inches, shattering on the far wall. In the same moment he heard a noise on the stairs, someone taking the steps in jumps. Bringing his bow up in panic, he loosed an arrow that took the woman between her breasts, just as she gained the landing. Her eyes bulged and she fell forward, her fingers scrabbling for his ankles, her bow falling from her hand. He shot her again in the neck. Impassively, he watched the signs of life ebb away, the blood pooling on the floor under her face. Before today, he thought, he had never killed anyone. Again, the silence closed in.

After this, nothing happened for a very long time. The sun rose in the sky, the day grew warmer, and twice he caught himself drowsing. They were doing exactly as he would do, he thought grimly. Far easier and safer for them to wait for him to tire, given the difficulty of his position for them. The blood on the floor was beginning to dry, and his wounded leg was throbbing painfully. He did not seem to be losing much blood. He shifted, trying to get more comfortable, and the afternoon wore on.

Abruptly, jerking him back to full alertness, there was an outburst of noise in the street outside, simultaneously downstairs in the building. Human shouting, screaming, the snarling of what sounded like a large animal. More distantly, the wails of cats. His eyes widening, fear cramping his stomach, he got to his feet, back to the wall, bow drawn. He snatched a glance out of the window over his shoulder, lowering the bow despite himself, amazed at what he saw.

Two women were in the street, half running, screaming, a sea of cats about their feet. More of the animals clung to their backs, their heads, clawing for their eyes. Something moved in a doorway across the street, and there was a snarl, and a scream that died away. Further up the street, two more human figures broke from cover, pursued by cats, running. He watched them recede into the distance, followed by the nearer women, the cats falling from them, and again the silence closed in. Very softly, once more, there came a noise on the stairs. His hand tensed on the bow. Then, gently, incredibly, came a cool touch in his head, so that he knew what would happen an instant before it did.

"Don't shoot me, Max, it's me."

Amazement surged over him. Trudie, here. Unharmed, despite everything. He closed his eyes for a moment, leaned back against the wall, shock and reaction hitting him at once. When he opened them again she was standing before him, her face drawn, her eyes full of concern, her bow in her hand.

"You're hurt," she said, guilt filling her voice.

He shook his head slowly.

"I can't believe you're here."

"I was nearly too late. They were bringing a ladder."

She took a step forward and took him in her arms, holding him against her. The scent of her filled him, and again their minds washed through each other, the desperation of each dimming into a deepening knowledge that the other had survived, that there was still someone who would care, could understand. He could not stop himself from shaking, because he had not expected to see the day's end, and she held him for a long time. At length she released him, said:-

"Let me look at your leg."

"It's just an arrow wound. It's clean." He hesitated. "Will we be safe here?"

"I'll know if anyone comes." She put down her bow, turning to look with distaste at the dead woman on the floor, wrinkling her nose. "Sit down, let me look."

He pulled up his trouser leg, and she untied the blood stained scarf. The wound was less clean on the side where the arrow had emerged, but the bleeding had almost stopped. She hesitated.

"I think I'll just strap it up again for now. I haven't got anything much with me."

He nodded, watching her as she bound the leg up again with some strips of clean cloth from her pack. He saw the lines round the mouth, the lines and dark circles under the eyes, the weariness with which she worked, with which she brushed back a loose strand of hair.

"Trudie, are you all right?" he asked softly.

She turned and looked at him, despair and hopelessness swimming in her eyes.

"No," she answered almost inaudibly. "Not really." She finished strapping his wound. "We can't ever go back, now."

Silence fell between them. At last he said:-

"Why not? What will you do? It's too dangerous here. And even you would die in the forest in the winter."

She nodded, her eyes brimming with tears, then she said:-

"He took Tammi, and I wasn't there."

He could think of nothing to say, so he reached out, hesitantly, for her hand. The force with which she held it was painful.

"What could you have done?" he asked gently.

"Killed him, perhaps."

"That would change nothing. You know what happens to killers. You still couldn't have gone back. It couldn't be undone."

She shook her head, hopelessly.

"I always knew he would, one day. I have for years. I should have been stronger. I should have made sure I was always there."

"No one could have done more." He looked at her. "I know what trying to keep her safe has cost you."

"If I'd been there he might not have done it. I'd always been good enough before."

She sat down beside him, staring across the room, over the dead woman's body, still holding his hand.

"He was asleep when I came in," she said. "I lit a candle and went to her room to check, the way I always do, even if she's asleep." She shuddered, her grip on his hand tightening. "He'd locked her in, the way he used to do to me, but I found the key."

Hesitantly, he put his arm around her shoulder, drawing her to him.

"At first I thought she was dead. She was lying on her bed naked, not moving, staring into space. There was blood from her all over the sheet, on her legs. She must have fought him, she was all scratched. Her breasts, her thighs, all bruised." She turned haunted eyes on him. "I didn't fight him, Max, I never screamed." She shuddered. "I just lay there."

Again, he found that words were beyond him. He felt his vision blurring with tears.

"I wasn't there," she said again.

He could think of nothing to do but hold her, rest his cheek against hers. After a long time she broke the silence.

"It reminded me of then," she said, very quietly. "When he first had me. I remembered the shame, the not being able to believe it. Wondering how I would keep it from Tammi. I remembered washing off the blood." She sighed, shuddering. "But I couldn't bear seeing her lying there like that, in the place where I should have been. My beautiful little sister." Again, her eyes met his. "I thought about killing her, then myself. Can you understand that?"

"Yes," he said. "I can. But you have to believe there's hope."

"Do you?" Again, her eyes filled with tears. "Max, you haven't seen her. She doesn't talk any more." She stared sightlessly across the room. "When you look into her eyes, there's no one there."

He held her, his eyes misting again.

"Nothing is important any more," he said at last.

She nodded.

"Yes, that's how it feels. But it was different for me, because I always had her to care for."

"I know it was different. I know why you never screamed, why you didn't fight him. Why you never thought of yourself."

She shook her head sightlessly.

"She was always so full of life."

"You held yourself together for her. What would have happened to her if you'd died inside?"

She sighed, turned her tear stained face to his.

"I would have died, this time, and her with me. If there hadn't been you."

"You are so beautiful and courageous, only you can't see it. It was you who saved my life again, today."

There was a long silence. At last he asked:-

"Where is she?"

"Not far from here."

"Is she safe?"

"Yes."

He got painfully to his feet, torn muscles crying out in protest.

"We ought to get her," he said. "Get away from here. Those people might be back."

"Not for a while," she said softly. "I saw the fear in their minds as they ran."

He hobbled over to the woman's body, pulled his arrows from it, wiped them on her clothes. They shouldered their packs and quivers, took up their bows. His leg had become very stiff, and she had to help him down the stairs, past the body at the bottom. He left the arrow in the man, its shaft broken as he fell.

The sun was bright out on the street, the animals had disappeared as if they had never been. The man and woman he had shot outside lay incongruously, sprawled where they had fallen. Trudie leaned on the wall by the doorway, eyes closed, face intent.

"It's safe," she said.

A crow flapped noisily away from one of the bodies as Max walked across to it.

Methodically, he recovered and cleaned his arrows. Turning back to her, as she stood by the door in the sunshine, he was touched again by the way she stood, by the exhaustion on her face.

"Go on," he said. "I'll watch behind."

Wordlessly, she led off up the street, past the building he had been surprised in. For a moment he thought of going back in for his pipe, resolutely put the thought from him. As they walked, his injured leg became less cramped, though a little more blood was seeping from it. Trudie turned left after a couple more minutes, entered a small building under tall trees. He thought he saw movement in the shadows as they entered, but she did not hesitate. Shrugging, trusting in her insight, he followed her up the stairs, onto an open balcony, in the dappled shade of the trees.

Tammi sat against the wall in the corner, her knees drawn up under her chin, staring out across the street with an unfocused gaze. At first glance she seemed the Tammi he knew, the same girl who had come to the smithy yard, it seemed so long ago. He watched the sun flecks playing across her tanned limbs, across her shoulders, her hair. He watched Trudie put down her bow, bend down beside her sister, gently touch her shoulder.

"Tammi, I've found Max. He's here."

She made no response, staring out across the street.

"Max is here. Look."

She turned, then, and looked, but right through him, the blue eyes no more registering his presence than they did the wind. She sat there, chin on her knees, staring through him as if he did not exist. A chill passed through him, and he turned away, not wanting her to see his face. He gripped the parapet of the wall for a moment, his knuckles white, then turned back to Trudie, meeting her gaze.

"I'm so sorry," he whispered.

Again her eyes were brimming.

"What I can do, Max?"

"All we can do is look after her. Be with her."

"Why does she shut me out?"

"Not just you. Everything."

She nodded slowly.

"I remember the look that used to be in your eyes," he said. "The way you wrapped the emptiness round you."

"Yes. What you keep on the outside can't hurt you any more." She closed her eyes, opened them again. "But now I have you, to tell me what's real."

There was a long silence, then he said:-

"It isn't safe to stay here."

"No."

"And the forest isn't safe either, with the wolves."

She turned a shaded, enigmatic glance on him.

"Maybe the forest will be safer again now." She picked up her bow again, as if she had suddenly made a decision. "Can we come back up the Sound with you in the boat?"

"Of course." He hesitated, frowning. "If no one's found it. Back to the village?"

"No, no." She shuddered slightly. "But you could land us before you get there."

"Of course." He was still frowning. "But Trudie, how are you going to live in the forest, just the two of you, with her like this? Even if there were no more wolves?"

She was looking away, her eyes distant.

"I don't know," she said. "I'll have to think of something. I haven't any choice." She turned back to her sister. "Come on, Tammi. We're going up the Sound in Max's boat."

Tammi got slowly to her feet. Trudie took her hand, then paused, eyes closed for a moment, before looking back at Max.

"It's safe outside."

Out on the street again, they retraced their steps. As they came level with the building Max had first escaped from, Trudie stopped at the top of the ramp, a ghost of a smile playing across her face.

"Go on," she said. "Go in and get your pipe. It should be safe. We'll wait here."

He hesitated, turned wordlessly, limped down the ramp. Despite his trust for her, the back of his neck pricked as he entered the gloom between the stacks. Moments later, he was outside again, his bow shouldered, a length of pipe under each arm.

"I could feel you itching as we came past before," she said, still smiling. "Shall I carry one?"

He grinned.

"Keep your bow ready," he said. "These aren't very heavy."

Twenty minutes later, and without incident, they were down at the Sound. He climbed the wall with difficulty, grimacing at the pain, relieved to find the boat as he had left it. He had doubted his chances of ever finding his way back through the forest, with the wound to his leg. Within minutes, the pipes loaded, they were forging out across the water in the sunshine, Tammi sitting motionless in the bow.

Max watched Trudie watching her sister. He saw the pain in her, the deepening lines round her eyes and mouth, and his feelings for her broke within him like a wave. He knew that she saw it, as she turned to him, tears in her eyes again, reaching for his hand.

"I can't believe you're still here," she said. "That you want to be with us." Her voice was very quiet. "I know you understand, but I still can't believe you do."

"You, of all people, should know."

She looked down at where her hand rested on his on the boat's gunwale, droplets of spray glistening on it.

"I'm a mess," she said, still looking away, her gaze momentarily unfocused. "Being with me may cost you, maybe even more than you think. I told you I can't look after anyone who matters. Max, I don't want to hurt you."

He shook his head, smiling slightly.

"You're all there is for me, now."

"Then there's the seeing," she said. "It saved us just now." Her eyes widened, the blue of the Sound behind her. "Who am I, Max? What am I?"

"I don't know," he said slowly. "Or what *I* am. But I do know that you're the only one who will ever really know me."

The boat sailed on, as the light played on the water. After a while she reached out and gently touched the fading bruise on his cheek.

"Did you get that in the Ruins too?"

He looked at her, the sun striking flecks of amber in his eyes.

"I went to visit your father before I came down here."

"Why?"

He sighed, spoke very softly.

"People had heard Tammi. Screaming. I had to know if you were both in there. Trudie, I had to know."

She closed her eyes, opened them again, looked back at him.

"Did he beat you?"

"He made a start. Fortunately for me, Oz had followed me, and had come prepared. I hadn't dared. I knew I would have used the bow on him if I'd brought it."

"Is Oz all right?"

"Your father was drunk, or it mightn't have gone as it did. Oz cut him, knocked him down. We bound it up and left him on the floor." He shrugged. "Oz will have been watching his step since. He'll kill your father if he raises a hand to him again, and won't much care how he does it. He's learned from what happened to Jez Yates."

"It can't go on, Max."

"It'll go on, as long as people let it. There are always going to be people like him, who enjoy power over others."

Trudie looked at Tammi, then out across the water, her eyes narrowed.

"Look at her sitting there," she said. "I will never, ever forget or forgive him for that. One day, I will make him pay."

The flatness of her voice chilled him.

"You're both still beautiful," he said.

"Maybe on the outside."

"You know I can see deeper than that."

She shook her head slowly, looking back at the slight figure of her sister, against the distant mountains across the Sound, and silence fell between them for a long time. At last she spoke.

"I have to go back there," she whispered, half to herself. "One last time."

Eight

Preoccupied by the events of recent weeks, Max had sought to lose himself in work since his return from the Ruins. Trudie had disinfected his arrow wounds in the boat, had dressed them with some of her herbs, and they were clean and healing well. He had successfully built and fitted the pressure relief device for the gas generator, and had then gone on to run a spur of the pipe into Oz's kitchen, to give him the option of cooking with gas. After a day's experimentation, he had found that drilling holes near the end of the pipe admitted enough air to allow the gas to burn with a blue flame, and he had spent the previous afternoon casting a burner in copper, incorporating what he had learned, and brazing it into a hob. He had sat back, satisfied, watching a pan of water heating over the flame.

Much of the work had been repetitive and manual, however, and at these times his thoughts had kept returning to Trudie and her sister. He remembered the return voyage from the Ruins, her asking him to land when they were still some two hours' sailing out from the village. He had put in to a small cove, the boat's bow grounding gently on fine shingle, and she had helped him pull it up onto the beach. He had been brooding about Tammi and her condition for most of the previous day as they sailed north, watching the suffering on Trudie's face as she watched Tammi, sitting, turned in on herself, in the bow. So he had asked her again if she suspected that Tammi might be like him, might be able to meet her in her mind. He had found it strange, given their closeness as sisters, that Trudie had said that she didn't know, had never tried, had never asked her. But then he had thought that perhaps there were things that she was afraid to give away, afraid to ask, afraid to see too clearly, and suddenly it seemed less strange.

So he had hesitated for a long time before making his suggestion, concerned at what it might cost them both. But, as he sailed the boat, his gaze kept being drawn from the sea and the mountains to Tammi, then back to Trudie watching her, and he knew he had to ask. So at length, hesitantly, he had reminded her of what had flowed between them in her father's barn, and then in her cave, when she first came into his mind and touched him. Then he had asked her what she thought would happen if she reached out to Tammi in this way, risking all, showing her everything; showing her that she herself had been where Tammi had been, that she understood, that strength could somehow come out of hopelessness.

At first Trudie had shaken her head, looking away across the sunlit water to the far shore. He had been uncertain whether she feared for herself or for Tammi, though, thinking about it now, he felt sure that it had to be both. There were so many uncertainties, just in respect of Tammi, he thought now, to the point where he almost regretted having spoken; the shock of finding her sister in her head, unexpected and unprepared for, the shock of learning, in detail as intimate as her own memories, of what had been done to Trudie.

Trudie had fallen silent for a long time, watching the forested slopes glide past, and then she had roused herself, sighed deeply, said that she would try when they landed, that after all there was nothing left to lose.

So they had sat down together, the three of them, on the fine shingle beside the beached boat, and Trudie had closed her eyes, turned her exhausted face up to the sun. And he had sat there, one hand in hers and one in Tammi's, and had felt her wash into his mind. Had felt the everyday mist away, tears starting to prick behind his closed eyelids, as he found himself in a girl's body on a rough bed, while the man came to her time after numberless time, running his hands over her, degrading her, using her like a dirty cloth, satisfying himself inside her. He washed away the blood, his eyes red raw from crying, he tried to wash himself clean, he gave up trying to wash himself clean. He had felt the deadness colouring into hate, mostly hate for self, because it was simply inconceivable that things like this could be anyone else's fault. He lived through the night when everything cracked, unable to bear the memory of the pain, as the whip laid itself across his back. Met himself under the pines in the morning sunshine, inexplicably offering relief, solace, coming to know, in the end, how he and Tammi had somehow provided reason for living, for going back, for enduring.

He had come to himself curled on the shingle, his body shuddering, with Trudie asking him over and over again if he was all right. She had sat him up, held him to her, and shame had filled him that it should been her comforting him, after she had bared her heart to them in this way. But he could not help himself, because he found it unbearable that anyone, above all her, should suffer like this, should have to bear such pain, such negation. He had known that she saw it, known that it gave her strength, as what had shaped her faded from his mind, and he began to hear the wavelets on the beach once more.

And Tammi had still been sitting there in icy stillness, apparently untouched. He had had no idea, when he suggested this, how much it would cost him personally, and it seemed inconceivable to him that it could have left her unmoved. He had begun to gain some idea of the distance to which she had gone away, of the strength and instinctive guile with which she had walled herself off. Trudie had given no indication of how deeply she must have felt Tammi's lack of response, saying nothing. She had sat hugging her knees for a long time, staring wordlessly out across the water, watching the light dancing with narrowed eyes. He had longed to reach out and touch her, and had somehow felt he could not.

In the end they had had a little to eat, and Trudie had taken her pack and bow, hugged him once for a brief instant, and had led her sister into the forest. She had not looked back, and in moments they had vanished between the trees. His emotions still raw, he had packed up his things, strained to push the boat off the beach. The breeze caught the sail as he hoisted it, and he had come on up the Sound to the village.

This morning, the gas burner working, he had felt the need for space, to sit and think. Oz was away to one of the farms, checking some shoeing he had done the previous day. Max had taken his bow and a little food, had headed out down to the river, past the mill and over the bridge, to the crag by the washing pool. Later, thinking about it, it seemed to him that it was only his distance from the village which saved him from injury or even death. He was walking beside the river, picking his way over the fallen rocks under the crag, heading for a ledge where he sometimes sat, when it happened. An excruciating pain lanced through his head, as if his skull had been split by an axe, and the world ignited into blinding light. He fell forward, already unconscious, his mind on fire, as the light hazed towards grey. He was not even aware of his body hitting the ground.

Trudie had left her sister in a place she thought to be safe, and had gone out into the morning. Shreds of mist were still lingering up the valley, between the trees. She went down to the river, splashed her face with water in a calm, brown pool, briefly inspected her reflection. Then she stood up, shouldered her bow and quiver, crossed the river at the boulders, began to make her way downstream. She hesitated at the falls, thinking of Max, of the tentative way he had touched her bruised face, of the look in his eyes, wondering if he would understand. She sighed, and lowered herself into space over the crag.

On the flatter ground below the falls, she settled into her easy run, and soon the cultivated land opened up before her, the village lying on the flood plain before the Sound, under a thin mist of wood smoke. She paused then, at the start of the track, her hand straying to her bow, to the tooth marks the wolf had left in it. After a moment she walked on down the track.

One or two people were about, as she came in among the houses, greeting her incuriously or darting furtive glances at her, according to their nature. Despite the general perception that Joss Taverner's business was safer ignored, there had been much talk in corners about screams in the night, followed by the complete disappearance of both his daughters. She smiled faintly to herself, supposing that her reappearance was bound to elicit interest, more, she thought bitterly, than the reasons for her disappearance ever had. So she came to the door of her house, gently tried the latch. It opened, and she went in.

She paused for a moment in the hall, taking in the familiar smells, listening. A noise came from the kitchen. She moved down the passage, cat-like, stood in the doorway, looking into the room, at her father's broad back, turned to her. Though she made no sound, some sixth sense must have warned him of her presence, because he turned to face her.

"So," he said, with barely a flicker of recognition, "you're back."

"No," she said softly. "Not really."

He appeared not to hear her.

"What have you done with your sister?"

"How do you know she's with me?"

Abruptly, he flung the knife he had been using at her. She shrank back against the door frame, and it clattered on the flagstones out in the passage.

"Don't play games with me, bitch," he snapped. "Where is she?"

"In the forest. Somewhere safe."

He advanced a couple of steps towards her, and she made to retreat down the hallway.

"You can stay over there, or I can run," she said. "Your choice."

He hesitated, unused to controlling his anger, knowing she was out of reach.

"You'd better bring her back," he said, "or it'll be the worse for you."

"I will never bring her back. Not after what you did."

He shrugged.

"Something died inside her on that night," Trudie said. "She doesn't speak any more. How could you have done that, especially after what you did to me?"

"She's probably more use to me than you ever were."

Trudie bit her lip, fighting the temptation to reach for her bow, but he took her anger as weakness.

"Admit it," he taunted. "You know you wanted it, right from the start. You led me on, the way you looked at me, the way you walked. Even before your mother died. Now you can't stand being put down for your sister. Women are all the same."

Torn between despair and fury, she was at a loss for words.

"You know I'm right, don't you?" he said. "After all, I know you. I know how your mind works. I know you've been seeing that dwarf. I expect he's all that'll look at you, now I've finished with you, and word's got around."

Her knuckles whitened under her skin, against the rough wood of the door frame.

"All I care about is her. I'd have gone away from you into the forest, years ago, if it hadn't been for her."

"Like hell you would," he sneered. "You knew which side your bread was buttered. You wouldn't last a fortnight in the forest."

She remained silent, knowing how little truth there was in that, though it would be different in the winter.

"I'll tell you why I took her," he went on, "since you ask. First, because she's mine, just as you are, and I can do what I like with what's mine. Second, because there's something the matter with you. Not just that you can't give a man any pleasure in bed. I wanted children by you, sons that I can hand this place on to."

She stiffened, but he went implacably on.

"God knows how many hundreds of times I wasted my time with you. I even checked when your periods were, thought about the time. It made no difference. There's something wrong with you."

She felt as cold as ice, gripping the door frame as she stood, and still he went on.

"There's nothing the matter with me," he said. "I had you two with your mother, before your sister ruined her, didn't I?" He looked at her, eyes narrowed. "You're useless to me, now," he said. "You mean nothing. Nothing at all."

She stood immobile, eyes locked with his. He half smiled.

"I enjoyed that night with her," he said. "There's always that freshness the first time, even if she's fighting you, even if you know what it looks like, even if it is your own flesh and blood. There's something beautiful about that."

Something seemed to snap inside Trudie, there was a red mist before her eyes. Anger and hatred blazed up within her, she wanted to reach out for him, to drive both her clenched fists together into his face. There. Her arm was going up for her bow, but abruptly the man was staggering, his face a contorted mask of pain. Both hands went up to his head, and he screamed, a ragged sound that suddenly chilled her. He staggered again, twice, and then, as if poleaxed, fell heavily forward, not trying to move or protect himself, striking his head hard on the flagstones. She thought she heard something crack. He twitched once, convulsively, and lay still. It was suddenly very quiet. She could hear a blackbird singing in the eaves outside.

Trudie stood, as if paralysed, in the doorway. She looked around her, but nowhere did anything move, in the room, the passageway, or outside the windows. She stood there for a long time, unable to move, watching her father, half afraid of a trick. He did not even seem to be breathing. At last, slowly, hesitantly, she took the few steps towards him, reached out her hand. He was not breathing, he had no pulse.

She leaned back against the table, her hands shaking slightly. She darted a glance out of the window, down the street, and her eyes narrowed slightly. She could see someone lying in the street outside, by the gable end of the house opposite. Quietly, she turned and went back down the hall. She had left the front door ajar, and she pushed it open a little, quickly looked up and down the street. She could see another body lying, a few houses along, though this one was moving slightly. She drew back into the hall, her breathing uneven, her mind working furiously, trying to understand.

She knew how it would look to people who wanted to see it a certain way. She had been seen coming to the house, the wronged daughter, then the dead father would be found. There was no obvious cause of death, but the rest would fit. There was little justice in the village, but the immutable principle that murder, irrespective of provocation, was always punished by death had prevented most of the worst excesses for generations. She knew the way things would turn, as she leaned against the wall in the gloom of the hall, and wondered about her premonition, as she came across the fields, that she would never see this place again.

After a long time she roused herself. She collected another pack from her room, packed it with a set of her own and a set of Tammi's clothes. She got her other bow, all her arrows, her father's long knife, which she fixed to her belt, and the spare bow strings. She took the flints from the barn, a bag of tinder, a bag of Max's fish hooks. She paused, checking that she had her own and Tammi's warmest clothes. Then she took her bedding and her last few possessions out into the farmyard. She stood for a moment, looking at the sad little pile, then she brought fire from the kitchen and set her things alight, standing and watching while they burned.

When only embers remained, she shouldered the pack, the bows, the arrows, put the last few clothes around her shoulders, and stepped out into the morning, uncaring, now, who saw her, uncaring of what anyone thought.

She walked away from the house, up the main street towards the forest. There was hardly anyone out, unusual in itself at this time in the morning. The three or four she did see were all sitting on the ground, holding their heads, a couple of them moaning as if in pain. If they registered her presence at all, they gave no sign of it. She hurried past them, up the street, towards where the fields began, leaving the village behind her, her face creased by a frown.

Max awoke, groaning, rolling over, a blinding headache driving a blade through his skull. The sun was dipping towards the Sound, and his limbs cried out with cramp. Slowly, mechanically, he rolled again, sat up. One side of his face, one arm, were badly sunburnt. He must have been out for at least a day. He was lucky the crows had not had his eyes. He groaned, rubbing his face, shielding his eyes from the sun. His bow still lay beside him, his arrows and food were still on his back. He sat there, massaging life back into his cramped legs.

After a long time he got to his feet, hobbled down to the river, bent and splashed his face with water. The ache in his mind was less like headache than the agony of torn muscle. He shook his head, looking down at the water foaming over the stones, remembering. Gingerly, he felt his head, but there was no wound, no bruise. He shook his head slowly, wondering. At length he gathered up his things, began to make his way down towards the mill bridge.

It did not take him many more minutes to reach the village. He was surprised, when he did, to find it almost deserted save for women, children, and old folk. Oz was in the smithy, though, using the gas flame to work some iron. He released the bellows with a start, stood up as soon as he saw Max.

"Thank God you're here, Max," he said. "Where have you been?"

Max frowned.

"Lying out by the washing pool, I don't know how long. Something happened, something knocked me out." His frown deepened. "I don't understand it, Oz. There's nothing wrong with me."

The smith's eyes narrowed.

"Something weird happened here yesterday morning. A lot of people here took ill around then. Headaches, couldn't see straight. Like getting hit on the head." Oz looked at him. "I felt it, here."

Max nodded wordlessly.

"Yes," he said at length. "It felt like that. But you're saying I was out for a day or more."

Oz was still looking at him.

"It was worst near the Taverner place," he said. "Some people out for hours there, in terrible pain when they woke." He came out from behind the forge, stood looking at Max, and sighed. "And Joss Taverner dead in his kitchen, without a mark on him."

"Taverner, dead?"

The smith nodded.

"Trudie was seen going in earlier," he said. "It all added up one way." He reached out, put his hand on Max's arm. "Stu Bell got the men together. They've gone out after her, into the forest, with dogs." He met Max's eyes. "This morning."

Max let his bow fall to the floor. He sat down heavily in his seat by the window, his mind working woodenly. He knew how it would end, now; Trudie without freedom of movement through Tammi's incapacity, and the men out after them with dogs. They would kill her out there, he knew, and bring her body back to the village as an example. What would become of Tammi, up there and afterwards, he could not imagine.

"I'm sorry," Oz said.

After a long time, Max met his gaze.

"You aren't out there with them," he said. "All the men join a hue and cry."

The smith shook his head slowly, looking down at the floor.

"I know what she means to you, Max," he said. "But it wasn't just that. Something told me this isn't right." He looked up again. "I don't know if she killed him. But I know enough to think she had cause, if she did." He sighed. "I couldn't persuade them not to go, but there was no way I was going with them."

"She had cause all right." He stared sightlessly at the floor, remembering the look on Trudie's face as she faced the wolf, a single stone in her hand. "She maybe did do it, Oz, though I wonder if she meant to, even knew that she could."

"There wasn't a mark on him."

"No." He shook his head almost imperceptibly, thinking again of her face as she confronted the wolf, knowing now, with sudden certainty, the way things had gone. "There was something of her in whatever hit me, down by the river." He hesitated, remembering the intensity of the pain, whose vestiges still lingered behind his eyes, and he shivered. "Power." Again he hesitated. "Oz, it nearly killed me."

The smith shook his head.

"You're losing me now, Max."

He shrugged, wearily.

"Then explain it to me, if you can. How he died. What you say happened to everyone here, especially near the Taverner place. What happened to me, even though I was further away."

Silence fell between them. After a long time, Max spoke.

"She didn't deserve it to end like this," he said softly. "All she ever asked for was life. For herself and for her sister." He gazed across the room, his eyes unfocused. "It just took too long for any of us to notice, or care enough to move. A little longer than she had."

"You did more than anyone."

"Not enough, though." He reached for his bow, getting to his feet. "I have to go after them. If they haven't got her yet, I may be able to get a couple of them before they get me. Buy her a little time."

Nine

As Oz moved to restrain him, men's voices sounded in the street outside. Max's eyes met Oz's, as the door of the smithy was roughly opened. Stu Bell pushed in, followed by Joe Rust, Mik Lundgren, and the others. Max backed into a corner, Oz behind the forge, picking up an iron as he did so.

"Come to reckon up, have you?" he asked. "Since I wouldn't play your little game?"

"There'll be time for that later." Bell's face was angry, his voice full of frustration. "We want to know what you know. You not coming with us looked bad enough before this."

"What do you mean?"

"We lost her scent. I still can't believe it. Just above the falls."

"That's right," Rust broke in. "Something drew the dogs off. A fresher scent they were more interested in. Kept getting false trails. We've been going in circles for hours."

Max realised he had been holding his breath.

"I reckon she expected this," said Bell. "She'd left nothing of hers in the house, to give the dogs her scent." He looked at Oz and Max in turn. "She killed her father. You hide her, you associate yourselves with that."

"How could I hide her?" Oz answered. "I've been here all the time. And even Joss Taverner admitted that I kept my nose out of his business, unlike some."

Bell turned back to Max.

"What about you, then?"

"He's been lying down by the river all day," Oz broke in. "Unconscious." He pointed. "Look at his face. He didn't know about any of this until I told him, a few minutes ago."

"What happened?" Bell asked Max.

"I don't know. Something knocked me down, but left no mark on me." Max looked around the brooding circle of faces. "I don't understand it. Oz says some of you felt it here."

There were nods around the circle. Bell frowned.

"It didn't knock any of us out," he said. "Except near the Taverner place."

Max shrugged.

"You asked me what happened."

"You can get heavy if you like." Oz let the iron drop noisily. "We can't tell you any more than you know already."

Bell appeared to come to a decision.

"I think he's telling the truth, lads," he said. "We have to find her first, bring her to justice. We'll meet again at sunrise." He turned back to Oz. "Once we've dealt with her, you can explain to the village why customary justice applies to everyone but you."

He pushed out through the door, the others following. Outside, it was getting dark. The forge's flames flickered on the walls, and it was suddenly very quiet. After a long time, Oz spoke.

"Do you know where she is?" he asked.

"No. Where she might be, perhaps. But she isn't stupid, and I've been wrong before." He looked at the smith. "Oz, why are you sticking your neck out for me?"

"I've been thinking of what you said before you went round Taverner's. About being sick of pretending shit doesn't happen."

Max grasped his hand.

"I owe you," he said. "Again."

"Forget it." Oz picked up the iron he had dropped, placed it by the forge. "Let's have some food. You can't have eaten since yesterday."

Though they never normally did so, they closed the shutters and barred the door. Oz got out food and a jug of ale, and they sat down facing each other, the table and a single candle between them. They both ate for a while in silence. At length Max said:-

"I'll have to try to think of a plan. To draw them off her."

Oz looked up.

"Seems to me she's doing all right by herself."

Despite himself, Max grinned.

"True." The food tasted good after the day without any. "I'd worry less if it wasn't for Tammi slowing her down. And she's all Tammi's got, now." He looked across the room, eyes unfocused. "I know myself what sort of life Tammi would have, orphaned here and without Trudie. And it'd be worse for a girl."

"It's a bloody mess." Oz sighed. "But they're still better off without their father. If it weren't for the hue and cry."

"Yes." Max looked up at him. "She's like another person in the forest. She can look after herself, without him to remind her of how she's dirty, worthless. As he made her, only she can't see it."

"Maybe she did something about that, this morning."

Max sighed.

"Maybe."

Silence fell between them. After a long time, Oz spoke.

"Those two girls could manage that farm."

"Yes. But they won't be allowed to."

Again, they fell silent. At length, Max said:-

"You've brought a hornets' nest about your own head on my account, Oz. And hers."

"You aren't the only one that has to live with himself."

Max paused.

"Perhaps you ought to tell them the truth. About everything."

The smith looked at him.

"I wouldn't have believed half of it myself if it hadn't been you telling me. The Ruins. The wolves. Above, all, what you say she can do."

"The Ruins are easy enough to find. And the wolves will most likely find us, sooner or later." He gazed sightlessly at the table. "But perhaps you're right about what she can do."

"No one likes someone different," Oz said. "You know that. Worse, someone who can see into things, private things. And if you're right, she did kill her father. They won't be interested in whether she meant to, whether she had cause. They won't buy it, Max."

"No." Max shook his head. "I know they won't. But I don't want you getting in deeper, Oz." He met the other's eyes. "You could do well out of this gas business, on top of all your other work. Once they see how good it is to cook and heat with, they'll all want it." A touch of his old enthusiasm crept into his voice. "I'd dig a pit and line it with lime cement if I built another generator, so it'd be less affected by the winter cold. Nothing rots in the winter." He paused. "There's enough pipe there, in the Ruins, to link up half the village. No problem getting it, if you took a few boats full of blokes down."

"You've never told me your ideas up front before. Never told me where you get your stuff."

Again, they looked at each other.

"There's no telling where this'll end," Max said quietly. "You know I have to try to stop them taking her."

"I know you well enough."

"And I owe you, God knows how much. This could get the village off your back." He broke off for a moment, then went on: "We'll play it this way if we have to. And even if we don't, I should have told you this other stuff weeks ago, now that things are the way they are between us."

He spent the next few minutes explaining to Oz, with the aid of sketches, how to get to the buildings in the Ruins where he had found the pipe and the copper. The candle was burning low as he finished.

"I'll have to go before dawn tomorrow," he said. "I want to be above the Falls for them coming up."

"I know it's pointless to try and stop you."

"Don't worry," Max said. "I won't reveal myself unless I have to." He smiled faintly. "I'm as good in the forest as any of them."

"Remember they'll have dogs."

"I won't go the direct way, and I'll take stuff with me to lay a false trail."

The smith sighed.

"Better get some sleep then, Max." He got up. "And I'll keep hoping, tomorrow."

Max made his way to his bed in the corner of the smithy. He blew out the candle, and, exhausted as he was by the events of the day, sleep overcame him almost as soon as he lay down.

He woke, unwillingly, to find Oz shaking him gently. The shutters were open, and the thin light of early dawn was filtering into the smithy.

"You were sleeping like the dead," Oz said. "I knew you'd never forgive yourself if you slept over."

Max sat up, rubbing the sleep from his eyes.

"Thanks."

"There's something else," the smith said. "I wanted to warn you before you went. I've been awake for hours. There's been terrible screams in the night. Three times, quite close together, in different directions." He looked down. "I left the bars and shutters closed."

Max nodded slowly.

"I'll take care, Oz."

He pulled on his clothes, put some food in his pack, ate a little bread as he got his bow and arrows. Saying goodbye to Oz at the door, he let himself out into the dawn, closing the door quietly behind him.

The sky was brightening behind the hills to the east, the village absolutely still in its neutral light. A thin layer of high cloud blanketed the sky, and only a few solitary birds were singing. He hesitated outside the door, then hitched his pack up on his back, turned, set off up the street. His eyes darted about, looking for movement; he was well aware how it would look if he was seen up before dawn, today of all days, with his friendship with Trudie apparently common knowledge.

Something was lying in the street, he saw, by the gable end of the Pritchard house. As he drew nearer, he saw it was a man, lying on his face. Blood had pooled under him, had run into the gutter. Max bent over him, suspicion hardening into certainty. He rolled the body over, unable to suppress an involuntary gasp. It was Dick Pritchard, and his throat had been torn out. Max rolled him back over, but the open eyes, the expression of terror on the face, remained imprinted on his mind. The body was cold. Pritchard had clearly been dead for some hours.

Max got to his feet. Turning, he saw that the door of the Pritchard house stood open. He took a deep breath. He walked towards it, entered, stood poised in the hall. He was acutely conscious of his own breathing, the silence had the quality of glass. There was no one in any of the downstairs rooms.

Again he hesitated. After a moment he began to climb the stairs, tensing at each creak of the boards. On the landing, each of the doors stood open. Looking into the first, he saw Madge Pritchard sitting up in bed. Her face wore the same expression of frozen horror as her husband's, her nightdress and bedding were a mess of blood.

Max realised that his fingernails were cutting into his palms. He breathed out, raggedly, walked into the next room. Old granny Pritchard was on the bed in there, and the story was the same. In the third room he found the three children, all dead. Their bodies were in the corner, as if they had been trying to escape. None of the bodies had been worried or partly eaten. The wolf had stepped in their blood, and had left footprints on the floor. He stood and looked at the small bodies for a long time. At length he turned, went slowly downstairs, out into the street. He stood for a moment, eyes closed, breathing deeply, then looked round to see whether he was observed.

Up the street to the left, the door of the Rust place stood open. He approached it, hesitated, already suspecting what he would find. Entering silently, going down the passage, he saw Joe Rust lying in the corner of the kitchen. Like the Pritchards, he had been killed by a bite to the throat. He did not bother to go upstairs.

Coming out of the house, still moving inconspicuously and watching to see if he was observed, he left the village by the southerly track, up between the fields to where the forest began, his hand on his bow. At the edge of the forest he climbed a large tree, moved in the branches until he could command a view of most of the village, and settled down to watch.

Time passed, and the light of the rising sun broke over the crags on the other side of the valley, across the waters of the Sound. The forest was full of birdsong. The usual wildlife moved between the trees, three squirrels, a deer.

Smoke began rising lazily from one or two of the houses in the village, he saw the occasional sign of movement between the buildings. From his vantage point he could see all the routes up into the forest, even the most distant one to the mill bridge. He shifted, stretching cramped limbs. Nothing moved on the trails, no party of men with dogs. He frowned slightly, recalling again every detail of what he had seen in the dawn, remembering Rust and Pritchard among those who had come to the smithy the previous night. Time passed, and the sun rose higher.

Eventually, after what seemed hours, a large group of men appeared on the easterly track. His heart quickening, he shifted on the branch, his hand straying to his bow, watching. They were not moving as he would have if he had been following a fresh trail with dogs. They stopped frequently, the lead figures studying the ground as if tracking, the dogs reined back on leashes. He smiled faintly, looked intently around him, dropped softly to the ground. It seemed that the priorities had shifted.

Moving stealthily around the edge of the cultivated land, he came behind the men as they entered the forest, keeping them just within sight or earshot. He moved with exaggerated care, as he could see that the party was well organised and vigilant, with men, bows in their hands, keeping a careful lookout in all directions. His attention divided between watching them and keeping his own lookout, he thought about wolves.

So the day passed. As the hours unwound, it became clear that the search party's task was proving as fruitless as it had on the previous day. There were many places where there were good wolf tracks, good scent, but always they intersected with others, disappeared into the river, leading them in meaningless circles above and below the falls, around the crags. Max had never seen wolf tracks in the lower woods until the day when he found Trudie trapped in her cave, and he shook his head, wondering.

In anger and frustration, the men turned back towards the village as night began to thicken between the trees. Max watched them out onto the cultivated land, then worked his way back along the edge of the forest, an arrow ready on his bow. At the head of the southerly track, he climbed his tree again, waited for night to fall. Once it was properly dark, he came back down to the village, slipped, cautiously and unobserved, back to the smithy.

Oz was sitting waiting for him, and they barred the doors, sat down to eat. Max told him briefly of what he had seen. The smith had remained indoors all day, judging it better, in his compromised position, to avoid gossip, even though it seemed that the wolf attack had temporarily diverted attention from the search for Trudie. After this, they ate largely in silence, each going to his bed, by common consent, once the meal was finished.

Despite his weariness, Max lay fully clothed on his bed for a long time, staring into the darkness. At length he sat up, opened the shutter a crack. He gathered his bow and arrows to him, and settled down to wait. After a time the moon rose, bathing the buildings opposite in its silver light. He watched, and time passed.

Because of his narrow field of view, he did not see the wolf until it was almost opposite the window. It walked silently down the middle of the street, ears pricked, tail held horizontal. Max's heartbeat quickened, a shiver ran down his back. Silver in the moonlight, the animal stopped, raised its nose, looked at the smithy for a long moment. Then it turned, padded to the door of the Quinn place opposite. It paused on the step, hesitated, as Max raised his bow, trying not to disturb the shutter. The animal lifted the latch with its nose, silently pushed the door open, entered the house. Max sighed raggedly, shocked that they had not thought to bar the door, lowered the bow.

His heart racing, he got to his feet, silently crossed the floor to the door. Unbarring it as quietly as he could, aware that he was compromising Oz, he lifted the latch, slipped out, softly closed the door behind him.

He hesitated in the doorway, looking at the moonlit street. Opposite, the Quinn door stood open, but he could hear nothing. He took a couple of steps forward, out into the moonlight, his fingers taut on the bowstring.

Abruptly, a single scream sounded distantly in the night. He shivered, and as he did so something moved in the Quinn doorway, and the wolf stood on the threshold, looking at him, a few paces away. He could see a darker stain around its muzzle.

He felt an icy weight on his arms, knew in a shocked instant that he could not move, could not raise the bow. The animal's eyes met his, as they had in the high forest, the moonlight swimming in their amber depths. But this time, in that frozen instant, he saw fish moving like silver in a deep pool, smelt pine needles under his nose, tasted warm blood in his mouth. Incredibly, distantly, he felt Trudie, somewhere far away in his mind. The bow dropped from his nerveless fingers as the wolf came down the step towards him. It walked past him, close enough to touch, silently away up the street in the moonlight, looking back at him once.

He watched it until it was out of sight, then bent and picked up his bow with a shaking hand. He let himself quietly back into the smithy, closed the door behind him. Going over to his bed, he closed the shutter, laid his bow and arrows down on the floor, and got into bed. He lay there for hours, staring into the darkness, his mind working furiously. Eventually, the last of his energy gone, he fell into exhausted sleep.

A touch on his shoulder, shaking him gently, a whispered voice.

"Max. Don't be afraid, Max, it's me."

His eyes snapped open, taking in the tableau in an instant. The door standing ajar - he must have forgotten to bar it again after his confrontation with the wolf - and Trudie. Trudie, sitting on the edge of his bed.

"Shh," she said. "I don't want to worry Oz."

She had opened one of the shutters, he saw, and the grey light of early dawn was filtering into the smithy. He looked at her sitting there, her face framed by two loose strands of hair, at the look in her eyes, the one he remembered when she pushed his boat out onto the water, that day in the Ruins.

"You're crazy. What are you doing here?"

"Shh," she repeated, a finger to her lips. "Don't wake him."

He shook his head slowly.

"They've been out in the forest looking for you, to catch you and kill you."

"I know. I've been watching them, laying false trails." The ghost of a smile touched the corners of her mouth and eyes. "It's not that difficult when you can sense what they're planning." She paused, looking into his face. "You looked so peaceful, lying there asleep. I didn't want to wake you."

"Why do you take such risks? Why have you come here?"

She looked at him for a long moment, then she said:

"I'm going away from here, Max. With Tammi. Come with us."

"Where? Where are you going?"

Her eyes were like ice in the strengthening light.

"I don't know. Somewhere."

His heart was racing.

"Where? Where will you go?"

"Over the mountains."

"But you've never been in the mountains."

"I've got what we'll need."

"You don't know what's over the mountains. No one does."

"No." She fell silent, then repeated: "Come with us."

He let his head fall back, his mind working furiously, trying to come to terms with the implications of what she was saying. She looked down at him, her gaze like the dawn.

"You can't just go. What will happen when winter comes?"

She sighed.

"Perhaps we'll be somewhere safe by then."

"I don't know, Trudie." He shook his head, his eyes closed. "It would just be the three of us. This, here, is all I know."

She bent over him, kissed him gently on the forehead, her hair brushing his face, then got slowly to her feet. Their eyes met.

"Thank you for coming out into the forest in case I needed help, yesterday," she said. "I know what it might have cost you. I know how much I'm asking, now."

"So much is starting to come together for me here," he said. "But I can't imagine life without you."

"I'll leave at dawn tomorrow, from my cave," she said softly. "If you come, I'll see you up there. No regrets, whichever way you choose."

She was gone, into the dawn.

He lay on the bed for what seemed an age, staring up at the timbers of the roof, his mind in turmoil. He knew she was offering him what he had always dreamed of, at least in part, but also that she was asking him to abandon the only comfort and security that he had ever known. He knew the risks that he would be taking, if he went into the mountains with these two, that there was a good chance they would all be going to their deaths. He knew that he would not be as strong a traveller as either of the girls. He remembered what she had said about not being able to look after anyone who mattered, about not wanting to cause him pain. He sighed, sitting up on the bed, knowing that, despite himself, the prospect of losing her left him without any choice at all.

He pulled on his clothes, picked up his bow and arrows, put a lump of bread in his pack, and let himself out into the morning. Preoccupied, he walked through the still sleeping village, frowning, looking down at the ground. He took the trail to the mill, crossed the bridge, sat down under the crag by the washing pool to think. When, hours later, Di Cutler and Aly Griggs came down to the pool to wash clothes, his mind was made up. He watched Di and Aly whispering together, watching him, knowing that he had become an outsider again, through his association with Trudie. Gathering up his things, he made his way back down to the bridge, along the trail to the village. There were small groups of women at several street corners, talking in low voices. They fell silent as he passed, and no one greeted him.

The smithy was deserted, and he remembered Oz mentioning delivering some ironwork to one of the farms. Carefully, methodically, he spent the next couple of hours laying out items he thought he might need, then eliminating those which he thought, on further consideration, were likely to be less than essential. Both his bows, all his arrows, his warmest clothes. Firebox and tinder, needle and threads, fish hooks, lard, spare arrow heads, dried glue, twine. Compass needle, hand saw and axe. He was putting the items which remained into his pack when a shadow fell across the door.

"Oz."

The smith looked at the things on the floor.

"What's this, then?" he asked.

Max sighed.

"What we talked about, the other night."

"So you're going away with her."

His tone mixed regret with resignation, with acceptance of a decision made.

Max nodded.

"I told you I owe you."

"You've done me as much good. And I've had your company."

Each held the other's gaze for a moment, then Max said:

"I'll leave you the boat, with the other stuff. I won't need it, where we're going."

"Where are you going?"

"Into the mountains, to begin with. Then, who knows where."

The smith shook his head slowly.

"No one goes into the mountains."

"We'll do what we can."

Silence fell between them, then Oz said:

"These wolf attacks are terrible. Three more men, and their families, last night." He paused. "And Orrie and little Jess Yates, down at the mill. Jez was out night fishing."

Max looked up, shocked.

"Orrie and Jess? Dear God."

"You'll have to be careful, in the forest."

"Perhaps we'll be all right once we're away from here."

"Or maybe they'll stop, then."

Max looked up at him.

"Maybe."

Oz held his gaze.

"Be careful what you're getting into, Max."

"Yes." Max shook his head. "Orrie and little Jess."

Mechanically, he went back to loading his pack. When he had finished he straightened up, put it on his back. He picked up his bow and arrows, turned back to face the smith.

"I hope I see you again, Oz."

Oz managed a smile.

"Stranger things have happened."

Wordlessly, they embraced.

"Goodbye, Oz. And thanks."

"Goodbye, Max."

He turned, closed the door gently behind him, walked away without looking back.

Ten

Max walked down the street towards the Sound, as if going down to his boat. When he reached the shore, he made his way along the beach to where the forest began. Once in the cool spaces under the trees, he climbed the large oak and settled down to wait. He waited for hours, until the sun was dipping towards the peaks across the Sound, and he was certain he had not been followed. Then he dropped to the ground, and began working his way through the forest around the edge of the fields, aiming for the river valley to the north east.

He came down to the river just above the falls, the crags across the valley stained with warmth by the setting sun. He crossed the river there, and took a circuitous route up the far bank towards Trudie's cave. As the spur above it came into view, he saw a slender figure sitting high on the rock, catching the sunlight against the darkening eastern sky. She raised an arm, and waved once.

By the time he reached the foot of the spur, she had climbed down to meet him. She stood waiting for him, smiling in the evening light. She had let down her hair, and it spilled across her shoulders.

"You're here," she said simply.

"I don't know," he said, flashing a troubled glance at her. "I don't know where any of this will end. But none of it means anything, without you."

"I didn't want to persuade you," she said with difficulty. "I wanted you to choose. But I'm the same. You're the only one who can ever understand."

"I hope so," he said. "After everything."

She looked at him, saying nothing, the sun in her eyes.

"But you still came," she said at last.

"Yes."

"I told you I'm a mess."

"Yes."

After a long time she sighed.

"Tammi's no better," she said.

"How will she manage in the mountains?"

"I can't see what else we can do."

She took him up to the cave then, to where Tammi was sitting, to look through him with her empty gaze. They ate a little cold food, as Trudie dared not light a fire so close to the village, and, as night thickened under the crag, settled down to sleep on dried grass she had collected. Somewhere far away in the night a wolf howled, but Trudie did not seem to think it necessary for either of them to keep watch. Max shivered, too full of doubt to argue. To his surprise, he found that sleep came quickly.

When he woke it was fully light on a dull morning, and Trudie was moving about. She and Tammi had been ready to leave the previous day, so little preparation was needed. The three of them ate some bread, then gathered up what was to go with them. Max carried what he had brought, and some dried meat and a water skin which Trudie had given him. Tammi carried a pack but no weapons, Trudie her pack, two bows and quivers, and the coil of rope which Max remembered seeing earlier, in her cave. Trudie stood in silence for a moment, looking at her cave, then turned without a word and led the way down to the river. They crossed at the boulders, and Tammi followed her up the valley, towards the high woods, with Max bringing up the rear, an arrow ready on his bow.

Moving at an easy pace, they followed the river up into the hills, retracing the route they had followed on the day they first encountered the wolf. The river danced over the rocks, birdsong was loud between the trees, but Max could not shake off a growing feeling of apprehension, even despair. He knew that only half his heart was in this journey, this journey with no imaginable end, that was complicated by the presence of Tammi, and by his growing sense that, for the first time, there was unfinished business between himself and Trudie. Yet he knew that staying behind while she left would have been impossible for him. He sighed, looking up at the crag behind which they had met the wolf. They crossed the tributary of the river with some difficulty, then continued up beside the main torrent for a time. Trudie paused for a moment, shifting the weight of her pack on her shoulders, and Max got out his compass needle, noting the direction in which it pointed. Wordlessly, Trudie started off again, angling away from the river, climbing all the time.

They were walking under pines now, the ground carpeted with fallen needles. It sloped away from the crest on which they stood, trees on every side as far as the eye could see. The weather was dull, with low grey clouds crossing the narrow patches of sky above them, and wind moaning in the treetops. After a while it began to rain, sounding on the foliage and beginning to penetrate to the forest floor. Trudie seemed like Tammi, turned in on herself, looking only at the ground ahead.

They were climbing again, up a steeper slope scattered with occasional boulders between the trees. Once Trudie missed her footing and stumbled, striking her knee on a rock. She said nothing, regaining her balance and continuing to climb. Behind her, Tammi moved lightly over the broken ground, never looking beyond her sister's back. Again, Max sighed, pausing for a moment, his thumbs hooked under the leather straps of his pack. Though he still scanned the forest on every side, he now carried his bow and arrow on his back.

Trudie hesitated at the crest, and Max came up beside her. Ahead, the ground dropped steeply away, into dim half light between the trees. Somewhere in the depths, he could hear a river rushing over rocks.

Trudie spoke softly, almost to herself.

"Just the three of us, you said." She flashed a shadowed, hesitant glance at Max. "I feel so alone."

He shook his head slowly, not meeting her eyes, and she shivered, wiping rain from her face.

"This is all my fault."

"What is?"

"Everything."

He sighed, running a hand through his wet hair, watching Tammi standing immobile, gazing without focus down the slope.

"I told Oz, once, that all you ever asked for was life," he said. "For yourself and for her. You only ever did what you had to." Again, he sighed. "Until two days ago, perhaps."

She looked at him for a long moment, from haunted eyes, then turned away from him, pushing back a strand of hair.

"Come on," she said.

The wind was gentler in the trees, and the rain had stopped, though large, cold drops still fell from the branches. The air was full of the scent of pine, as Trudie led the way down into the ravine. The steep slope under the trees never caught the sun, and a profusion of ferns grew between wet boulders and slabs of rock, mostly covered in a sodden, slippery blanket of moss. Below, in the dim light, the river rushed. They made their way down carefully, faces turned to the slope, holding onto the rock. Once a fern came away in Tammi's hand as she put her weight on it, and only Max's sudden grab for her wrist saved her a plunge into the rapids twenty feet below. She made no response, her face turned into the rock, inches from her nose. He climbed down beside her, trying to keep close, seeing all too clearly what would happen if one of them broke a limb.

The rock steepened to almost vertical as they neared the water, and they had to traverse upstream for a little way, to where the river cascaded over a rock fall. Here there was both a flat area to rest, and a place to cross. Max watched Trudie sitting on the damp rock, watching the water foaming over the stones. Tammi was drinking from cupped hands, and after a moment he bent down and joined her.

The river came down the ravine over a series of waterfalls and rapids, and dropped away behind them through the trees, a tributary, he supposed, of the river which ran past the village. He watched Trudie get to her feet, pick her way across from rock to rock. They were large and securely bedded. Tammi followed, then Max, wiping his wet hands, climbing the steep earth slope on the other side. At the top the ground levelled off, sloping gently away again through the eternal pines. Max touched Trudie's arm.

"Should we have some food?"

"I suppose so." She hesitated. "Too wet for a fire."

"We can have some of the dried meat. And the rest of the bread I brought."

He divided the bread and a few strips of meat between them. Trudie watched him and Tammi eat, taking only a few mouthfuls herself.

"Don't you want any more? You'll need it, for energy."

She shook her head.

"I'm not really hungry."

He looked at her, at the detached yet intent look that stole over her face when she was out in the forest in her mind. He sighed, gathered up her uneaten food, returning it to his pack. Tammi had eaten hers, and now sat immobile, gazing out into the green spaces between the trees. At length Trudie roused herself, got to her feet.

"We ought to go on."

The ground was no longer broken, just a smooth, gentle slope under the pines. They walked between the trees, on the soft needles, for a considerable distance until the gradient steepened once more. Again, the faint rush of water sounded, this time the flow of a larger river. As they descended a long, sweeping slope into its valley, the trees began to thin out, some broadleaves interspersed now with the conifers. A brown, foaming river descended the wide floor of the valley in a series of cataracts, forest alternating with areas of open grassland along its rocky banks. Beyond the far bank the mountains rose higher, lost in the cloud, their lower slopes clad once more in forest. They finished their descent, emerging onto the grassy meadow beside the river. Trudie paused, looking at the river, and up at the sky.

"Could be good fishing," she said.

Max nodded, looking at the driftwood along the banks.

"We could make a fire here."

They put down their packs and weapons, and he spent the next few minutes collecting smaller, drier pieces of driftwood from sheltered spots among the rocks of the bank, while the girls used larger sticks to dig in the soft soil for earthworms. He got out his tinder box and flints, and in a little time had coaxed a fire into life. Returning to the river, he brought larger pieces of driftwood, and built and watched the fire until he was satisfied. Trudie was sitting on a flat outcrop of rock, fishing, and he saw that Tammi was fishing too, a few yards further upstream. He walked back to the river bank, sat down beside Trudie on the rock. She had two fish, he saw, rainbow trout. Wordlessly, she passed him a worm for bait, and he cast his line. He sat beside her, the sound of the river all around. The weather seemed to be brightening.

"Why did you ask me to come?" he asked at length. "You know you can travel faster without me."

She sat watching the river, the ever changing patterns in the current. It was a long time before she spoke.

"You always cared. You said I was everything to you, and you showed me it was true." She fell silent for a moment, then went on: "And you're more like me than like any of them, back in the village. We're different from them." She flashed a glance at him. "I told you last night, you're the only one who's ever understood. I think we're like each other."

"Those wolf attacks," he said, unable to help himself, having to go on. "Two nights. Eight men and their families, all killed. Just killed, not eaten or dragged away." He broke off, watching her. "I saw the bodies of the Pritchard children, together in the corner of their room. Three little bodies, each killed by a bite to the neck. I remember the look in their eyes." He sighed, still watching her face. "And Oz said Orrie Yates is dead, and little Jess. Orrie bound up my knee, fed me, only a few days ago. Do you still think we're like each other?"

She did not take her eyes from the river. At last he said:

"I don't know if I came with you because you seem to care, or because you're so beautiful to me. But part of you terrifies me."

Still she would not meet his eyes.

"I don't know anything any more," she said. "I didn't ask to become the way I am. I told you I'd only ever learned how to run, to hide." She shook her head, almost imperceptibly. "I don't think I know how to love. Then suddenly, you find you have power." She turned to him, the haunted look back in her eyes again. "I tried to warn you, Max, I tried to tell you what I'm like. I didn't want to persuade you to come, though I think you know how much I wanted you to say you would. I just couldn't have gone, not without telling you first."

"No," he said after a long time. "I'd never have forgiven you."

"Well, then," she said softly.

Again silence fell between them, broken by a bite on his line. Surprised, he almost lost his grip, but was able to play and land a brown trout. He watched it flopping about on the rock, the gills gaping, the eyes watching him. He cast his line again, then he said:-

"We've left everything we ever knew. And life was hard enough in the village."

"Oh, Max." For a moment she looked at Tammi, sitting immobile on her rock, then rested her chin back on her knees, watching the water moving. "Who would ever have wanted her or me?"

He felt the pain of his disability, and had nothing to say.

"Except you," she said softly. "That's really why I asked you to come. I don't think I can manage without your courage, your unselfishness and faithfulness, the way you laugh at your own pain. I need the way you look at me, even now, despite everything. Despite the last two days." He could hardly hear her. "I can't go on without that, whatever you may think of me now. That's why I asked you, and what I meant when I said we're like each other."

Again, he was unable to speak. She put her hand over his, where it rested on the rock. They sat like that for a long time, then she said:-

"Your fire's dying down. Come on. Let's cook the fish."

Tammi had caught two more fish, a young salmon and a trout. They took their knives and gutted them, returning the entrails to the river, and laid them in the embers of the fire to roast. The three of them sat round the fire in silence, enjoying the smell of the cooking, suddenly aware of hunger. They divided the fish between them, laying them on flat stones warm from the fire, eating the steaming morsels off the tips of their knives. Max finished first, wiping traces of oil from his lips.

"We could stay the night here, catch more to take on in the morning."

Trudie looked around her.

"This grass looks well grazed. If deer, horse, sheep, goat come down here, then so might wolf and bear." She paused. "I think we should cross the river and find somewhere safer."

He nodded regretfully, seeing the sense in it.

"I suppose you're right."

He kicked over the remains of the fire, while she threw the fish skins and bones into the river. A little downstream, the river ran wide and shallow. They shouldered their packs and bows, and waded across, holding hands to steady each other, their boots hung round their necks. Half way across, Trudie lost her footing, and Max's grip on her hand was unable to prevent her from sliding into the icy water. She was soaked to the skin when they reached the far bank, and stood wringing out her hair and clothes, as best as she could.

"Stop and change your clothes," he said.

"All my stuff's soaked too. I'll be all right. You can help me when we stop for the night."

He was worried about wind chill, but supposed that her clothes would dry on her if she kept moving.

"All right."

They began to climb away from the river, its sound fading. The slope was steep, but the pines were more widely spaced, and grass and heather grew between them. After a time the ground levelled suddenly and they stood on top of a narrow ridge, several hundred feet above the river. The light was beginning to fail, and ahead of them the higher mountains reared, much of them still lost in the cloud. In that direction the terrain became steadily more broken, ravines deeper, slopes steeper. They looked in silence at the huge rock masses under the cloud, knowing that their way lay between them. Again, Max got out his compass needle. They had travelled in a remarkably consistent direction all day.

They lay down to sleep for the night on top of the ridge, beneath the trees, huddled together for warmth, Trudie wrapped in dry clothes from Max's and Tammi's packs. She ignored his protestations about one of them keeping watch, repeating over and over again that they would be safe. In the end he saw that he had no choice but to trust her yet again. Weariness overcame him, and he was asleep before it was fully dark.

He woke as first light was breaking, cold and stiff from lack of shelter. A thin drizzle was falling, its greyness enveloping everything, and the mountains were invisible in cloud, clinging in shreds and tatters to the crowns of the pines on the lower hills, one with the rain. He sat up, shivering and hugging his shoulders, stretching stiff limbs. Trudie and Tammi lay together, both still asleep. Trudie's face seemed flushed, and her lips moved as she slept. He frowned, bending over her, touching her forehead gently. She felt fevered. Still frowning, he got to his feet, took up his bow and quiver, and moved silently off along the ridge, into the forest, warmth slowly returning as he walked.

About half an hour later he returned, carrying two rock doves, and a squirrel which he had surprised at the foot of a tree, his demeanour little improved by the loss of two arrows. As he neared the place where they had spent the night, he heard a sound, and froze, listening. Again the sound came, of someone retching. As he came into the clearing he saw that it was Tammi, kneeling on all fours under a tree, being violently sick. Laying down the animals, he knelt by her, put an arm around her shoulders, took her hand. She did not look up, gave not the slightest sign of recognition, but he thought he felt her fingers tighten around his. They were icy cold. He knelt by her for several minutes until the sickness passed, and she got to her feet, stumbling back into the clearing, to sit down next to her sister. To Max, slowly picking up the bodies of the animals again, she seemed like a discarded coat, like a husk or a shell. Trudie was still asleep, moving uneasily, her breathing irregular, her skin flushed. He sat down heavily, watching them.

After a long time he took his knife and gutted the birds and the squirrel, laying the entrails to one side. Plainly he would never get a fire started in this weather. He removed the livers, offering one to Tammi, but she turned away. He cut them into strips on a piece of wood, to save the edge of his knife, and slowly ate them, checking each piece for parasites. Then he skinned the squirrel and plucked the birds, spitted them on sharpened sticks, and hung them from a juniper bush, well clear of the ground.

The rain was heavier now, large drops sounding on the foliage, on the ground at his feet. He went over to Trudie where she lay, put his arms under her shoulders and legs, strained to lift her. There was no excess weight on her, but she was tall, and the task was almost beyond his strength. She moved, moaned, but did not wake. He managed to move her to a drier spot at the base of a tall pine, and Tammi came mutely over to sit beside her when he took her by the hand. He stood watching them both for a time, then got his little saw out of his pack.

"Tammi," he said, taking her hand again, "Trudie isn't well. We need to cut wood for a shelter. Come and help me. Walking will help you keep warm."

She did not look at him or make any response, but she got to her feet, still holding his hand. Together, they searched the forest nearby for fallen branches, which he trimmed with the saw, and she helped him carry them back to the clearing. She held them for him as he stacked them together, building a shelter over where Trudie lay, as he had done so many years ago when he found her, near to death, in the forest near the village. He took bracken stems and bound the branches together, then they used smaller sticks and leafy shoots of fresh pine, woven together, to fill the spaces, building it up into a reasonably weatherproof covering. Tammi did much of the work. She would not initiate any activity, nor respond to him in any way, but would work quietly for long periods of time if he told her what he wanted, and showed her by doing it himself. She seemed better now, despite her earlier sickness.

He left her to finish the shelter, then got the water skins from their packs. He went down the slope to get water from a spring he remembered seeing the previous evening, a few hundred yards down the slope, regretting bitterly, as he walked, his failure to persuade Trudie to change her clothes after falling in the river. There was no excess fat on her, he knew how easily she felt the cold, how poor her chances would be if this fever went to her chest. Returning to the shelter, he took a strip of cloth from the pack, wet it in the water, and bathed her forehead with it. She moaned, her eyes moving under the lids, but they did not open. He settled her on some of his dry clothes, and covered her with one of her furs.

Tammi had finished working on the shelter, and he led her inside too, where she would be protected from the worst of the weather. She drank some water, and took the remains of the bread when he offered it to her, eating slowly, turned in upon herself. He wrapped Trudie's other fur around her shoulders. Deep in thought, he took up his bow again, and walked slowly away between the trees, returning, after a few minutes, with an armful of smaller wood, placing it in the shelter in the hope that it would dry. He sat down on a log, head in his hands, wondering what he would do if he lost them, as the wind moaned in the pines above his head.

So the day passed. Cloudberries grew in profusion along the ridge, under the pines, and he spent the afternoon gathering them with Tammi. He was gratified to see that she ate some, and she took a little raw dove breast when they returned to the clearing. During the afternoon the weather brightened a little, and in the evening the setting sun broke through the thinning cloud, staining the higher mountains with with rosy light, though the forest around them lay in shadow. Max stood looking at them for a long time, captivated by the quality of the light, by the scale of the crags and rock faces, absolutely clear in the aftermath of the rain. Already larger than any he had ever seen, the mountains filled him with apprehension. Trudie's breathing was deeper and more regular now, and he moistened her lips with water, before lying down himself on the damp ground in the shelter, with Tammi between them.

Eleven

He stretched, turning his face up to the sun, then looked around, his eyes intently searching the forest. Turning at a sound from behind him, he saw that Tammi was awake, her eyes huge in an ashen face. She stumbled out of the shelter to the edge of the clearing, bending down and vomiting. He went over to her as he had the previous morning, held her until the spasms passed. This time she held more tightly to his hand, and their eyes met when she sat up. He thought he saw a momentary flash of gratitude, of life there in the emptiness. He smiled wearily at her, but withdrawal had closed in again.

Trudie was sleeping on her back, her breathing deep and regular. Her hand, when he touched it, was cool. He sighed, then shouldered his bow, and went down the slope to the spring, splashing his face in its icy water, and drinking deeply. He refilled the water skins, and brought them back up the hill. When he returned to the shelter Trudie's eyes were open, mirroring the sky. He bent down beside her.

"Max." She closed her eyes, opened them again. "How long have I been asleep?"

"A day and two nights. You had a fever."

She tried to sit up, but he restrained her.

"Lie down. Rest, until your strength comes back."

She let her head fall back.

"I'm sorry, Max."

She closed her eyes again. Fleetingly, he touched her hand, then got to his feet. He brought the sticks from the shelter out into the open to dry, then took his bow and walked into the forest along the ridge, returning in a few minutes with two more squirrels. He sat down to skin, gut, and dismember them, then he built a fire place from stones, started a fire with his tinder, carefully laid the smaller sticks on it. Some of the wood was still damp, and the fire was hesitant and smoky at first, but it gained in strength as the wood dried. He placed the larger wood by it to dry, and the spitted doves and squirrel from the previous day above the flames. When he turned, he saw that Trudie had sat up, and now leaned back against one of the poles of the shelter, the wind in her hair. She smiled faintly at him, closing her eyes.

When the meat was ready, he shared it with Tammi. Trudie would not take any, but to his relief she drank some water and ate some of the cloudberries. He put the animal skins on the fire, added extra wood, then piled up more stones. He had cut the squirrel meat into strips, and now he placed them among the stones, and heaped peat and wet moss up around the fire, hoping that it would make enough smoke to preserve the meat. When he looked at Trudie again, she was asleep, an expression of peace on her face.

That afternoon he went out into the forest again, coming upon a small herd of roe deer among the trees below the spring. As he worked his way around them, trying to keep down wind of them while getting close enough for a good shot, they must have sensed his presence. They burst off down the slope, white tails dancing between the trees, leaving him cursing. He had to content himself with three birds, at the expense of another arrow lost.

Trudie was still asleep when he returned, with Tammi sitting next to her, pulling the petals from some flowers she must have gathered. Laying the birds on the ground, Max sat down next to her, hugging his knees, watching a thin wisp of smoke coiling from the earthed up fire. As he sat there, enjoying the warmth of the sun on his skin, Tammi spoke.

"Max."

He jumped at the unexpectedness of it.

"Tammi."

He forced himself to go on looking at the fire, not to over react, though his heart was thumping painfully.

"We've left the village, haven't we?"

"Yes, we have."

"We won't ever go back there, will we?"

"No."

Her voice was like that of a little child, empty of expression.

"I won't ever see him again, will I?"

"No." He dared a glance at her now, out of the corner of his eye. "No, you won't. Not now."

She nodded slightly, her eyes closed, her face relaxing into an expression of peace, folding back into herself. Watching her, sitting trance like next to him again, he began to think that he had imagined her speaking.

Trudie awoke again in the late afternoon. She took some water and more of the cloudberries. Max unearthed the fire, removed and hung up the smoked squirrel meat, and cooked the animals' livers. She took a little of that too, and Tammi ate the remainder. Again, as dusk deepened over the ridge, the three of them lay down in the shelter to sleep.

Max woke to the sound of Tammi retching. He got to his feet, joined her where she knelt on her hands and knees a few feet from the shelter, taking her hand, putting his arm round the thin shoulders. Again, she gripped his hand, her fingers moist and very cold. She shuddered as the sickness left her, then looked up at him, her eyes the blue of the morning sky, up between the mountains where they had to go.

"Thank you, Max," she said softly. "For being kind to me."

He looked at her, unable to stop his own eyes misting, unable to stop himself smiling.

"You're back."

She nodded slowly.

"You said it was safe."

He looked at the pitiful pool of vomit on the grass, and then back at her.

"Go and wake Trudie," he said. "Talk to her. Tell her."

Tammi knelt by Trudie, gently touched her shoulder, whispered softly to her as her eyes flickered open. Though he knew he was not, Max felt like an intruder, a voyeur, at the look of joy that spread across her face. He watched them there in the entrance to the shelter, clinging to each other, both crying. Quietly, he took his bow and moved out into the sunlit forest, a new spring in his step.

They remained at the shelter for the next two days. Trudie was back on her feet on the first, going down to the spring and a little way along the ridge, but she tired easily, and suffered from dizziness, having to stop and sit down. By the second day her strength was returning, and she came with them to gather cloudberries. In the afternoons Tammi went into the forest with Max to hunt; she now carried Trudie's other bow. When they returned on the second day he had sat down beside Trudie, told her softly of Tammi's sickness the last four mornings. Trudie had looked at him, the haunted look back in her eyes again, and then had looked away, out across the forest, saying nothing. He had sat and watched her, his mind full of sadness, afraid of the long reach of the past.

Tammi was sick again the next morning, and this time Trudie woke with her, went to comfort her. Max unearthed the fire, and they breakfasted on the last of the cloudberries, and two rock doves killed the previous day. Trudie declared that she now felt well enough to travel, so they packed up and left the shelter, heading into the hills.

Midday found them well into the foothills of the mountains. The day remained fine, but the wind was fresh, moving in the short grass which covered the slope ahead of them. To their right a crag reared, the clouds moving past it dizzyingly. Ravens wheeled around the rock, their dry cries spinning down out of the blue.

Trudie had been leading, moving at an easy pace and resting frequently, conserving her slowly returning strength. Now she paused beside an outcrop of rock, running her hands over it. It was unlike any she had ever seen, pure white, crystalline, shining in the sun. She watched Tammi and Max, both standing with hands on hips, looking down the slope. It fell away for hundreds of feet, into a ravine where a stream rushed. Distantly, on the far slope, two stags moved. Beyond, the lower hills stretched out, as far as the eye could see, blanketed in forest. Cloud shadows moved serenely over the slopes, merging into blue haze, receding into the distance. Max turned to her, smiled too when he saw she had been watching him.

"How are you feeling?" he asked.

"Tired. But I'll be all right."

He looked past her, out into the distance.

"How vast the world is, when you see it like this."

"And us so small."

"Yes." He sighed. "We know so little of this high country. And autumn will be here in three months."

"We'll find somewhere safe."

"I hope so." He remembered Tammi's sickness, how quickly the weather could change, the fact that they only carried food and water for a day, and sighed again. It felt good to be out of the forest, but he wondered about the hunting on these open slopes, what the coming days and weeks would hold. Despite his years of independence, the enormity of what they were doing struck him again.

"We have to cross the mountains," she said at last. "After that, we'll see."

Shifting her pack on her shoulders, she started to climb once more. The brow of the slope hid the higher mountains from them, the green crest standing against the blue of the sky, a buzzard riding the wind above it. They climbed for some time in silence. Abruptly, the slope levelled off, and as they topped the rise the mountains unfolded before them, and a lake lay at their feet. It ran for miles between steepening crags which reared into the sky on either side, its waters cold even in the sunlight. Beyond the lake the valley narrowed, its precipitous walls closing almost to a cleft, in inky shadow between the first two immense peaks. Snow lay on both, despite the season, lending them a strange delicacy against the blue of the sky. Beyond them, other summits stood out, all clear of cloud now, a colossal wall running across their path, receding into hazy distance to right and left. Wordlessly, they stood looking at the mountains, a landscape on a scale that was altogether new.

A few minutes more found them down on the lake shore, wavelets breaking into foam at their feet. Max unshouldered his pack.

"Let's fish," he said. "Food may be scarcer higher up."

They stopped to fish for a couple of hours, sitting on some large rocks a little way along the shore, catching four small trout between them. Old, dry heather made an indifferent fire, barely allowing them to cook the fish. At length they moved on along the shore of the lake, following an animal trail. The crags fell steeply into the water, and the going was rough, with frequent scrambles over scree or through boulder fields, pushing through coarse heather, through bog where bright green moss grew. There were many small streams to ford, and it was late afternoon by the time they reached the head of the lake. Fatigue had suddenly struck Trudie, but all of them were feeling the effects of a day's walking, and all had wet feet.

They were already out of the sun here, as the crags drew together at the head of the lake, running up into the snows of the mountains. A chill wind blew down the ravine, and a stream rushed down its rocky floor, feeding the lake. Abruptly, Trudie sat down on an open platform of rock beside the stream, and Max was dismayed to see a tear run down her cheek.

"I'm sorry," she said. "I can't go on any more today." She shivered, laying her pack aside on the rock.

Tammi did likewise, sitting down beside her, drawing her knees up under her chin.

"What a hard, cold place," she said.

Max laid what he had been carrying down beside them.

"We'll have to stop here for the night."

The rock platform sloped gently uphill for perhaps thirty yards. Above it, a boulder field began. To the right was the foot of a scree that fringed the valley's wall, the stream to the left. He walked slowly up to where the boulders began, relieved to find that there were spaces between the rocks deep enough to offer some shelter. He went back down to where the girls were sitting, concerned that Trudie was still shivering, and brought them and the equipment up to the place that he had found.

They huddled between the boulders as evening drew on. The rocks provided some shelter from the unremitting wind, but the air temperature had already dropped, far lower than Max had expected, and he began to be concerned. When he looked at Trudie her fingers were blue, and Tammi was little better.

"We could die of cold in the night if we don't do something," he said abruptly.

Neither of them answered him.

"Grease and dry grass. Like the hunters do in the winter. Come on, help me. Get all your spare clothes and furs out."

He got out his little pot of lard, and Trudie roused herself with an effort.

"I thought of that, too." She searched in her pack, bringing out a pot of her own.

"All over your body," he said. "Not just arms and legs."

They loosened their clothes, teeth chattering with the cold, and rubbed the fat on. Trudie and Tammi helped each other, and Trudie covered Max's back. Her fingers were like ice. Then they dressed again, each putting on all the clothes they had. They went and gathered dry grass from below the rocks, the movement helping restore some warmth to their bodies, and stuffed their clothing with it. Despite her weariness, Tammi began to giggle at Max's and Trudie's appearance, and it proved infectious. They put more grass in their packs, twisted yet more together into twine, tied the remaining furs around themselves. By then it was almost dark. Returning to the shelter in the boulders, they took off their wet boots and socks, put their feet into their grass filled packs, and lay down on the cold rock to try to sleep.

When Max did sleep it brought little comfort, filled as it was with travellers' dreams of mountain lions and bears, the ever present cold, the sound of the wind around the rocks. As dawn began to break he saw with dismay that the sky had clouded over. At first he was so stiff that he had difficulty in moving, but slowly the life returned to his limbs. He pulled on his wet socks and boots and got gingerly to his feet, rubbing greasy hands together. His fingers were almost too numb to tie the laces. Minutes later Tammi awoke, to her usual sickness. He crouched next to her between the rocks, holding her to him, as she retched helplessly. They went down to the stream together, to splash their faces with water and drink a little. Trudie was awake, sitting up, when they returned.

Max refilled the water skins, and they chewed the remaining few strips of the smoked squirrel meat. It was hard and acrid to taste, but did not seem to have rotted. They gathered up the few things they were not wearing, shouldered packs and bows.

Trudie was looking up the course of the stream. The valley narrowed to a deep ravine, in places little more than a cleft between two immense walls of rock.

"There isn't any other way, is there?"

Max looked at the mountains on either side, sweeping up to the snowline.

"I wouldn't give much for our chances on snow, after last night."

They began to follow the stream up into the ravine, between precipitous walls which soon hid the lake from their view. The going was rough and painfully slow, as they often had to walk on stones in the bed of the stream. Several times they had to scramble over what were plainly recent rock falls, eyeing the cliffs above them with apprehension. It was cold and sombre in the bottom of the ravine, the clouds moving dizzily across the narrow strip of sky between the crags. At length the ravine split, but the tributary did not seem to offer any easier going than the main channel, with a smaller stream descending a series of waterfalls, an almost unassailable wall of rock.

After this large boulders filled the channel, piled randomly, each having to be clambered over. The rock was rough, crystalline, hard on hands and knees, but at least the effort was bringing warmth back to their bodies. Trudie appeared recovered after her night's rest, and let the way, with Max bringing up the rear. Now she stood atop a boulder, dismayed at what she saw.

"What's wrong?" asked Max.

"Come up here and look."

Ahead, the stream plunged over a near vertical drop of some forty feet.

"It's impossible."

"Wait." Trudie stood, hands on hips, intently examining the rock. "There's a way up there, to the left."

"It's so dangerous. What if one of us falls?"

"No," she said, her voice growing in confidence. "It'll be all right. I'll show you."

She crossed the stream, and they followed her to the base of the fall. There she took from her pack the coil of rope she had brought from her cave, and some clips, softly shining, made of a strange, light metal unfamiliar to Max.

"I got these in the Ruins. And found out what they made them for. Look."

She showed them how to tie the rope into the clips, run it round their bodies under their arms. Explained how they would stay roped together, one climbing and the other two securing the rope, in case any of them fell. She would lead, going not more than ten feet or so before Max followed her up, so that the height she could fall would be limited. Max was smiling, impressed, as she finished.

"How do you know all this?"

"There were some drawings on a wall in the high Ruins, where I found this stuff. Old and faded, but you could still see. Other things, too." She broke off, remembering. "I wish we had some of them, now."

"What made you bring them?"

"I just thought it might be useful to know how to climb." She smiled, half to herself. "I thought it looked like fun."

"Fun." Max grinned despite himself. "Right."

"Are you ready?"

They nodded. Max paid out ten feet of rope, and Trudie began to climb. He watched her moving up over the rock, her face pressed against it, searching out finger and toe holds, marvelling at her quiet confidence, her concentration, at the strength in her fingers. After a few moments she paused at one end of a ledge, wedging her back into a crack, and looped the rope about the rock.

"Come on up then, Max."

She had made it look so easy, but it wasn't, not at all. He tried to tell himself that he had scrambled on rock many times near the village, but there the holds had been obvious by comparison, close together, large enough for most of a hand or foot. Some of them, here, would have escaped his attention if he not seen her use them. Another problem was that he lacked her reach, so that he needed additional holds between hers. It was several minutes before he joined her on the ledge, out of breath, his palms moist, feeling foolish.

"Secure the rope," she said. "I'll climb on, then there'll be room for Tammi to come up while you wait on the ledge."

He waited while she climbed, his face pressed against the rock, trying not to look down at where Tammi stood, watching. When, moments later, Trudie called down, Tammi came easily up to the ledge, with much of Trudie's natural grace. Max smiled ruefully at the rock.

Some minutes later they stood beside the stream at the top, Trudie coiling the rope and returning the clips to her pack. Max and Tammi were looking up the slope. They were clearly close to the snowline here. The stream now ran in an open, shallow depression between the mountain walls, between rocks shattered by frost. The only vegetation was scattered patches of moss and lichen. As Trudie made to pick up her pack, Max motioned for stillness, and his hand went slowly to his bow. He loosed an arrow, and a bird moved suddenly between the rocks, pitching forward into stillness. When he picked it up it was a type he had never seen, mottled brown with two white bars on each wing. Better, it had been sitting on a nest. They cracked the four small eggs, swallowed the contents, and Max tied the bird to his belt, shaking his head when he found that the arrow had broken on the rock.

Eating the eggs had only made them more aware of hunger. After some time they came to the stream's source in an immense boulder field. Ahead, the slope eased, climbing to a pass between two ice covered peaks. Their height was dizzying, dwarfing the mountains at the head of the lake when Max looked back.

A brisk wind was blowing as they picked their way over the boulders up towards the ridge. The sky above them was clear, but thunderheads were forming to the east, and cloud lay on some of the summits ahead of them. After some time, chilled by the wind, legs heavy with weariness, they reached the saddle. The ground fell away gently before them, dropping away into an upland valley in the near distance. To Max's relief, the country ahead of them seemed to be at somewhat lower altitude.

It was too cold to stop and rest. The descent steepened as they went, and the valley unfolded beneath them, nothing but thin grass covering its slopes. Trudie, leading, stopped suddenly, on the edge of a huge space.

"We can't go down this way," she said.

She stood silently, peering intently over the edge, her attention fixed on something. Approaching with caution, Max saw that the rock fell sheer in front of her for hundreds of feet, tailing out into scree.

Trudie had bent down, was uncoiling her rope, getting out two of the clips. She fixed the end of the rope round a rock outcrop, took a loop round her body, clipped in. Caught unawares for a moment, Max had failed to register what she was doing.

"You said we can't go down that way."

"I'm not. Hold the rope for me."

A turn of rope around her leg, she stepped backwards over the edge. Max motioned Tammi to stay back from the cliff edge.

"Trudie, don't be stupid," he called. "What are you doing?"

"I'll be back in a minute. Please don't distract me. See the rope stays secure."

Within five minutes she reappeared at the cliff edge, unclipping from the rope, taking three large grey eggs from the bag at her waist.

"Food," she said simply.

Looking down into the valley, his head swimming with vertigo, Max knew that the short journey would have been beyond him.

"Why didn't you say what you were doing?"

The faintest of smiles touched her lips.

"We both know what you'd have said."

Twelve

Max slumped back against the rock, his head full of the ceaseless thunder of the river, his eyes closed against the sun, his mind freewheeling. He was no longer sure how many days it had been since they had crossed the high saddle between the ice peaks, how many days of unrelenting cold, how many days since they had eaten the last raw remains of the bird he had shot. Certainly two full days shrouded in cloud, the wind plucking at his compass needle and flicking sodden hair in his eyes, as they picked their way forward through blinding greyness, soaked and chilled to the bone. The wind rising to a howl during the second night, as they huddled in a cave that was barely an overhang, their stomachs cramped by hunger, the air sizzling with lightning and static. The ear splitting, rending sound of nearby strikes, Tammi's hand in his, squeezing so tightly he thought his bones would break. Then the river they had come upon as the weather cleared, rushing fast and deep in a rocky gorge, cascading over falls, barring their path. Quite impossible to cross, forcing them higher still into the mountains, or else to do the unthinkable, and turn back. He thought this must be the second day with the river to his left, and now, exhaustion permeating his whole body, he was thinking how easy it would be not to go on.

A shadow fell across him, a gentle touch on his shoulder.

"Come on, Max," Trudie said gently. "There's nothing for us here."

Shielding his eyes from the sun, he forced himself to his feet. To the east, the sky was clear, revealing a panorama of mountains, peaks stretching to north and south as far as the eye could see. They walked for what seemed hours beside the river. Grass could barely grow at this altitude, giving way to rock, lichen, moss, and other small plants with which they were unfamiliar, and once again they had seen no life all day, save distant birds and a pair of mountain sheep, watching them from under a crag, far out of range of the bows. The unaccustomed combination of hunger, vast open spaces, and brilliant sunshine lent the world the quality of hallucination. A sense of unreality closed in on Max, walking behind Trudie and Tammi. He and the two girls' backs seemed all that moved under the huge arch of the sky, they and the ever present river to their left, rushing over rocks, throwing the sunlight back at him. The sound filled his mind, almost drowning the noises their feet made on the rocks. Walking on the broken ground required total concentration, and it grew still harder as the hours passed, with the hunger, weariness, and the unrelenting brilliance of the sun. When Tammi stumbled and almost fell, twisting her ankle slightly, they stopped abruptly, sitting down beside the river to rest, eyes narrowed at the intensity of the light. Max sat a little downstream, Trudie between him and Tammi.

"I feel faint," Tammi said. "I can't go on much longer."

"Oh, Tammi." Trudie put an arm round her shoulders. "You know I haven't any food to give you." She turned to Max, who was staring sightlessly into the rapids. There were tears in her eyes when he looked at her.

"What are we going to do?" she asked.

"What can we do? Keep going, as long as we can."

She lowered her voice.

"I couldn't bear anything to happen to her."

Max sighed.

"This is what I was afraid of. We don't know what lives here, even if anything does. We don't know the ways of the animals, what plants there are. You're right when you say we can survive in the forest, but up here -" He broke off, shaking his head, looking back at the river.

"It isn't just that." She moved closer, so that she could speak without Tammi hearing over the sound of the rapids. "It's her sickness, Max. I have to face up to it."

Hopelessness swam in her eyes as he looked back at her.

"I'm sure she's pregnant," she said.

They were silent for a long time. At last, he said:

"I thought you knew. After you had the fever, in the forest."

She shivered.

"I don't know what I'm going to do. It's his. The child will be his. Our half brother, but also him, living on. Reminding us. Reminding her. What will it do to her, mothering that? Looking at it, years later, and seeing him?"

He could think of nothing to say.

"How can I tell her, Max, after everything?"

He was thinking that they might easily die here, that perhaps it would be better if death found them, but he said:-

"Perhaps she knows. She isn't stupid."

"You can know something, but not want to see it."

"Yes." He fell silent, then he said: "There are ways of losing a child. I heard the women talking about it."

Suddenly she was sobbing, holding him, her eyes tightly shut. Seeing them there, Tammi got shakily to her feet. To Max, the depth of love and concern in her eyes suddenly, irrationally, justified any amount of pain.

"What's the matter with her, Max?" she asked.

His courage failed him, and he said:

"She's worried about you, Tammi, that's all."

He left them in each other's arms, got out his fish hook and line, and fished while they sat there, talking softly to each other, but he caught nothing. Standing on a boulder, looking up the valley, he saw that about a mile away the main course of the river turned to his right, deeper into the mountains. When they started to walk again, the slowness with which the girls moved filled him with unease, and he knew he was no stronger himself.

As they neared the bend in the river they were forced to climb, as the spring floods had cut into the side of the hill. Their progress was painfully slow, but at last they came to the crest above the river bend. He could see Tammi's legs shaking with weariness. The river cascaded down a cataract above the bend, and above that the valley widened, below where it emerged from the higher mountains. Here the river's course was braided. It flowed steadily, more slowly, in a host of smaller streams, separated by gravel flood plain. Trudie's eyes met his, a trace of hope back in them.

"Look. We can cross there."

In another hour they were down on the flood plain, fording the many streams without incident, the icy water nowhere coming higher than their knees. They paused in two places to fish, but caught nothing; Max suspected that the falls further downstream had kept fish from ever reaching this part of the river. Eventually, their stomachs tight, water skins refilled again, they walked away from the river at last, up a gentle slope, as the sun dipped towards the hills behind them. As they climbed the slopes, stopping frequently to rest, they saw that the river had its source in a great lake, sunk in a depression in the mountains. The snow covered peaks along its sides seemed to float, insubstantial, their flanks lit by the setting sun.

The sun dropped below the horizon before they reached the ridge, and the chill was abruptly back in the air. In a few more minutes the ground levelled out, then fell away before them for thousands of feet, in tier upon tier of hills. At their foot lay an upland plain which receded, in the gloom of the evening, almost as far as they could see, fringed by distant mountains on both sides. In the east, where night was already gathering, Max thought he could see another range of lower hills. Trudie stood, as if carved from stone, gazing out into the dusk.

"That way will be easier than staying in the mountains."

Max ran his eyes down the nearer slopes.

"It'll take us most of a day just to get down there. Trudie, somehow we have to find food."

"I know." She sounded unutterably weary. "I know."

"There's no cover anywhere. I don't see how we can hunt, even if anything lives down there. And no plants you can eat." He fell silent, hunger and fatigue making his head swim.

"It'll be so cold if we stop here," said Tammi faintly. "But I can't go on."

Rounded hills ran for miles on either side of them, offering no shelter at all in the near distance. In the end they descended a little further over the short, wiry grass, until the failing light and the weariness in their legs made it difficult and dangerous to go further. Both girls, with their fairer skins, were quite badly sunburnt, and Max smeared the remains of his lard on their foreheads, noses, lips. Then they lay down together on the grass, Max and Trudie curled up on each side of Tammi, huddled together for warmth. Max lay awake for hours with hunger cramping his belly and the cold seeping into him, thinking about love and loss, of commitment and its cost, falling eventually into fitful, exhausted sleep. And Trudie sat up then, shivering, her eyes brimming with tears, trying not to cry as she watched him finally slip into sleep beside her sister, the Milky Way bright above them.

When Max awoke it was early dawn. The air was windless, the huge flank of the mountain painted in neutral shades, absolutely still. He was shivering uncontrollably, as if the cold had penetrated into his very bones. It had been a calm, clear night; a heavy dew lay on the grass, and the temperature could not have been far above freezing. He rolled over, suddenly seeing it, suddenly struck rigid at the sight of what lay a few feet from him: the body of a mountain sheep, its eyes open in death.

His eyes fixed on it, he reached for his bow, then paused, searching the mountainside in all directions. Painfully, he got to his feet, went over to the body of the sheep, examining the wounds to its throat, looking intently at the markings in the soft ground around it. He exhaled gently, shaking his head. Wolf kill, here. Fresh, but no longer warm. He sat back on his heels, thinking furiously, not, in his heart, entirely surprised. He remembered Trudie's conviction that there was no need to keep watch, back in the forest, the way she had been prepared to leave Tammi alone in the forest, in the Ruins, and what Oz had said about the wolf attacks.

He went over to Trudie, took her hand, cold even in his. Watched her, anger, mistrust, and tenderness fighting for a place on his face as the cloud shadows do over the mountains, as her eyes flickered open.

"A wolf left its kill in the night," he said.

She breathed out slowly, looking up at him, watching him.

"We had to have food."

He nodded, wordlessly.

"It'll help us, in the days ahead."

"Yes."

"I was sure you knew," she whispered. "From what you said already."

He looked at her.

"Remember what you said yesterday? About knowing something, but trying not to see it?"

She avoided his eyes.

"Yes."

She was shivering, her lips blue. She rolled over and sat up, and impetuously, despite himself, he put the fur he had been wrapped in round her shoulders.

"Trudie, look at me."

She stared down at the ground.

"Look at me. If you care at all."

Reluctantly, she met his eyes. He saw the fear and desperation swimming there in the blue, and he remembered what she had said about being too wounded to love.

"I've trusted you with my life. Why couldn't you tell me? Right from the start?"

"I'm sorry." He could barely hear her voice. "I've spent years never telling anyone anything. Trying to manage by myself, though now I know I can't. Then it was too late, after what I'd done. I knew I would disgust you. I know what I'm really like." She shivered, her chin on her knees, looking away down the slope. "I know what you'll think of me."

"I showed you what I feel, back there in the cave, but you still couldn't trust me enough."

"Oh, Max." She spoke almost inaudibly, her lips hardly moving. "You're a good person, you do what's right. I'm twisted, worthless, compared to you." She looked up at him, her eyes haunted. "You said I had courage, but it takes so much to really trust."

He fell silent for a long time, then he asked:

"Why did you kill so many of them, back in the village?"

"They were trying to kill me. For something I never meant to do."

"One, two, would have stopped them. You know it would have, with your intelligence and power against them as well as the fear. Why the others? The women, the children?"

She shuddered, looking away down the slope.

"None of them did anything, ever, for me and Tammi. They all knew, and they all looked away. I can see that now." She smiled, a twisted little smile, her eyes full of tears.

"Forgive me," he said. "It all seems so far away now, but I have to ask you about this, I have to understand. Because this is about whether you care enough to trust me with yourself."

She would not meet his eyes. When she spoke he could barely hear her.

"I care enough, Max. But I don't think I trust you not to hate me, once you really know me."

He hesitated, knowing that it was the way she spoke the truth that drew him to her, then he said:

"Why the children, Trudie?"

It was a long time before she could speak.

"It's about power," she said. "It's something about power. All your life you try to make yourself small, make yourself nothing, because your only defence against people with power is to be so small that they pass by you instead of hurting you. And then, just as they were ready to kill me, after a lifetime of that, suddenly *I* had power. Over them. And it was like a game." The words came in a rush. "So precise. So neat. I put the images into the wolves' minds, the peoples' faces, what the houses looked like. They're intelligent, they can tell the difference. I showed them how to open the doors. It all worked."

He said nothing. After a moment she went on, quietly now:

"I could do whatever I wanted. I used two wolves at a time, I only ever had two. I was in and out of their minds when they were in the village, telling them this one, that one, not that one." She looked at him. "Not you."

"I know. I felt you there."

"I know you did."

After a long time she went on:

"I was in the wolf's head as each of them died. I had to make sure. Each death was different, but each one was terrible, like the traveller in the high woods. Their fear was the worst thing, because it was always just the same as mine. I knew I was doing it, of my own free will, but I couldn't help myself, I couldn't stop." She flashed a glance at him, and there was only hopelessness in her eyes now. "It's shocking to see that in yourself. But Max, none of those women ever helped us. Don't you see, you of all people, they would never have had us back. Would never have let us marry their sons. We would never have, could never have, been as they were. Not after everything. Perhaps they always wanted to kill us. Or would have grown to."

"Perhaps," he said softly.

Silence fell between them, as Tammi slept on, her face touched by the first rays of the rising sun. Eventually he said:

"When did you get the wolves? You never even told me that."

"After he took Tammi. I took her up to my cave. I was desperate, I had nothing to lose. I remembered what you'd said about the wolves maybe being sensitive to me. So I called them, although I was terrified to after the time you saved me, and after a while two of them came. A dog and his bitch. This time I was ready. I used all the power and knowledge I had, everything I'd learned with the cats in the Ruins, with the other wild animals. It worked, and I won."

"So you had them in the Ruins, that last time?"

She nodded.

"I used them to help you, along with the cats. They killed two of the people. I saw the fear they caused."

He remembered the movement in the shadows in the house where they had left Tammi, recalled again her confidence about their safety at the cave, in the forest.

"And you used them to draw the dogs off, when they came out hunting for you."

Again, she nodded.

"It's quite easy if you know the ground, use their eyes to see where they are. The dogs were more interested in fresh wolf scent than the poor scent they had of me. It worked after the wolf attacks, too. I made the wolves keep following a complex route, used the water to break the scent, kept them well away from the cave." She paused. "Then they followed us when we left the cave, only came close at night to watch us so that we would be safe. It wasn't difficult for them, they can travel faster and further than us. They could have hunted for us every day, but I was afraid to let you see, after what you said by the river, afraid of what I knew you'd think." She paused again, sadness threading her voice. "The bitch is dead now, killed by a bear just the other day. Remember I found bear tracks the morning after the thunder? Because I forced her to help me." She sighed, shivering. "I ruin whatever I touch."

He made no reply, then after a long time he said:

"You use your seeing to play these games of yours, not to bring us closer. You open a door, a door that you say means so much, then you slam it in my face."

When she answered, she sounded near to tears again.

"Those 'games' were life or death for me and Tammi. And I never promised you closeness. Not because I don't want it, but because I'd probably be afraid of it anyway, and I know what being close to me would do to you. Look at us now. I don't deserve someone like you, Max. I don't deserve anything at all."

"I don't know. I don't think I know anything any more. But why Orrie and Jess, Trudie? Why them, last of all?"

She would not meet his eyes.

"I won't lie to you, Max. I can't change what I did now, God knows I would if I could. I knew that every time I killed one of them, especially the children, it was so wrong, but I had to start, because I knew I couldn't hide from them much longer. Once you start, you don't know where you should stop. I wondered if it would work outside the village, further away." Her voice had fallen to a whisper. "They were furthest away. I should have stopped at their door. But I didn't."

For a long time neither of them spoke.

"I know I was wrong," she said. "I know I've done more wrong, now, than any of them ever did to us. And I will suffer for it. I can see what you think of me. I know I deserve nothing. I know that what's happened has put me out of reach, even of you." She rested her head in her hands. "I knew it would."

He was unable to say anything, unable to deny a single word. After a very long time, he spoke.

"I could have forgiven you everything," he said softly, looking out over the distant plain, as the sunrise broke across it. "Because you've endured so much, and you're so beautiful, even now. But Orrie and Jess, just to see if it worked. I don't understand, Trudie. I just don't understand how that could have happened."

Wordlessly, he got up, took his knife from his belt, and began to skin the sheep, his back turned to her. He worked like that, going on to gut and butcher it, for what seemed a very long time. He heard Tammi wake, he heard Trudie go to comfort her in her sickness, but he did not turn, did not pause in his mechanical working. There was nothing to turn round for, nothing else in the world at all.

Thirteen

It was the same for many hours. He could not bring himself to react to her, relate to her in any way. He sat a little way from them along the slope, gazing out across the plain, turned in on himself. Tammi came over to him after a few minutes, her face furrowed by worry, concerned that something terrible had happened while she was asleep. He was moved by the depth of her care for him and the fact that none of it was her fault, but it could not melt the ice in him, his feeling of betrayal, that what had meant so much to him now seemed to wear a different face. He told her that Trudie would tell her about it, but did not try to hear whether she did, what she said. After a little more time Tammi brought him a piece of the sheep's liver, and he took it and ate it, but could barely keep it down, despite his hunger.

Shortly after this they moved off down the slope, Trudie and Tammi together, Max a little way behind, carrying as much of the sheep meat as they could. The sky was clear of cloud, and the slope they were descending caught the rising sun and sheltered them from the wind, so that warmth soon returned to their bodies. They walked almost in silence, Trudie and Tammi exchanging occasional monosyllables, Max in his own world, staying twenty or thirty feet behind. After some time Tammi dropped back, waiting for him. As he came level with her she took his hand, looking anxiously into his eyes.

"You've been kind to me, Max, though you owed me nothing," she said. "Please talk to me."

"I'm sorry. I didn't mean to upset you."

"Why are you angry?"

"I'm not really angry. Or maybe I am, but at myself. I just need time to think." He sighed. "I told you, ask Trudie. She'll explain it better than I can."

"I did ask her," she said. "She said that at last you'd seen what she's really like, inside, and that it had shocked and hurt you. She wouldn't say any more." She watched him, seeing the pain on his face. "Max, I've seen how much you care for her. I don't want it to be like this."

He walked on beside her, not meeting her eyes.

"There's been so much pain," he said at last. "I'm sorry, Tammi. This has nothing to do with you."

"It has, though," she said softly. "There's only the three of us now, and we're all bound up with each other. All I want for her is that she should be happy, because she's given up everything for me. As you have, for her."

He looked at her then, at the precocious wisdom and understanding in her eyes.

"Some sort of peace is all I ever wanted for her too," he said. "Because it seemed to me that she deserved it, more than anyone I've ever known. But I don't think I really understood how deep the wounds go in her. I thought I had enough courage to love her, whatever she thought or did. But how can I be talking to you like this, Tammi, after what happened to you?"

"Don't worry about me," she said gently. "You've both helped me, as much as anyone ever could. Remember when she tried to show me it all, everything that she'd gone through, most of it on my account, that time down by the Sound? So that I'd understand, and not feel so alone? You both thought I didn't see it, but I did. I know how much I owe her, and I saw what happened to you, when she was showing me." There were tears in her eyes now, but she was smiling at him. "I saw how much you cared, and it helped me carry on. I thought, if there are people like Max in the world, then maybe it'll be all right."

For a long time he was unable to speak. At last Tammi said:

"She needs you so much, even when she can't see it. You're all there is for her, Max, the only one she's ever dared to let close enough. Without you, all that's left is darkness."

"You're not like that," he said. "Even now. Even after what happened."

"Only because she was always there, shielding me."

"But never anyone to sheild her."

"No."

Again they fell silent, walking on. He watched Trudie walking down the slope a little way ahead, the pack and bows on the thin shoulders, stooped now with weariness, her hair matted with grease and dirt. The memories welled up in him, the light in her eyes, the wind in her hair, the scars, the forbearance, the courage. Tammi's hand tightened on his.

"Thank you for for being here, for us both."

He sighed.

"She still means more than the whole world to me."

"I needed to hear you say it was still true."

They walked in silence for a long time. At last she said:

"There are only the three of us now, but next year there'll be four. I'm going to have his child, aren't I?"

Remembering how painful anything less than the truth could be, he simply nodded.

"Thank you for not lying to me," she said. "I've been sure, for days." He wondered at the strange calm acceptance in her eyes. "Trudie knows, doesn't she?"

"Yes. She couldn't bring herself to tell you." He hesitated. "Talk to her. Tell her you know."

"I will." She looked up at him. "You will help me, Max, won't you? When the time comes, and afterwards?"

"You know we both will."

"I'm going to walk with her now, and talk to her."

He watched her catch up with Trudie, fall in at her side, take her hand. He watched the sisters walking together, talking, Tammi's head against Trudie's shoulder, thinking of what Tammi had said about caring, shaking his head once. After a little time they came down into a dry, shallow valley, before the next rank of foothills fell away towards the plain, and abruptly Trudie stopped, still looking in front of her, and Tammi walked on a little way, stood poised, not looking back.

Hesitantly, he came up beside Trudie. He hesitated again, then slowly, uncertainly, he took her hand.

"I am so sorry," she said, very softly. "I will suffer for what I've done."

"I'm sorry too." He sighed. "Because you were right not to trust me."

Wordlessly, she turned to him, took him in her arms, pressing him against her. They stood there for a long time, neither of them able to see the other for tears, in some sort of affirmation. He knew that there was a difference between acceptance and forgiveness, though perhaps not a very large one, and he knew that she saw it too. When, at length, they walked on, each of them reached out a hand to Tammi.

It was late in the afternoon by the time they came to the bottom of the lowest range of foothills. The afternoon was hot, as the wind had rolled what little cloud there was back towards the mountains, and the air was mild at these lower altitudes. Little forest grew on this side of the mountains, and Max wondered about rainfall and the availability of water. Here, however, up against the hills, there was a spring and a grove of ancient thorn trees, and they were able to fill the water skins and gather sufficient wood for a fire.

Concerned about the sheep meat keeping fresh in the warmer air, they built the fire up and roasted everything they had, eating their fill of meat and fat. Earthing up the fire, they left the rest to smoke. It was uncomfortably hot, their bodies more used, by now, to the cold of the mountains, and they had all stripped to the waist, the girls untroubled by modesty.

Trudie did not even try to hide her back. They sat next to the smoking heap of the fire in the shade of a thorn tree, looking out across the plain with half closed eyes, enjoying, at last, the twin luxuries of warmth and full stomachs.

"I thought we were going to die in the mountains," Tammi said at length.

"We were lucky to get through it." Max shifted against the tree. "I'm still wondering how easy it will be to hunt down here. And what might hunt us."

Trudie opened one eye.

"The wolf will still help us," she said. "To watch at night, and help us hunt if necessary." She closed her eyes again, turning her face up to the sun. "It's coming down through the foothills now."

On the other side of her, Tammi was rubbing her arms and legs. Then she started laughing, an uninhibited, infectious sound after the privations of the previous week.

"I am *so* dirty," she said. "I don't think I've ever been so dirty in my life. I wonder if I'll ever be clean again."

Turning to look at her, Max had to agree. Streaks of the insulating fat they had used in the mountains covered her arms, legs, face, body, breasts, ingrained now with dirt. Blood from the sheep had dried on her hands and forearms, and her hair was matted and lifeless. She untied it, trying to shake it out.

"I'll never get a comb through this."

"Have you got a comb?"

"Of course."

She sounded surprised. He turned away, smiling, meeting Trudie's eyes.

"Actually, I brought it," she said. "We girls have to think of our appearances."

He was laughing at her now.

"You didn't bring a mirror, though." He wiped at a streak of grease on her cheek with his thumb. "Probably just as well."

"I'll settle for still being alive," she said.

He propped himself up on an elbow, watching her.

"So what happens now?"

"Maybe we'll find somewhere to settle down beyond this plain."

"I'm worried about water. I couldn't see anything from the mountains, as we came down."

"How far do you think it is?"

He bit his lip, frowning.

"Maybe fifty, sixty miles, to those hills we could see when we came over the mountains?"

"M'm. Three, four days if things go well. We'll just have to carry as much water as we can, try to drink it slowly. Maybe rest in the heat of the day, if it's this hot, and if there's shade. There are plants here, it isn't a desert. And we've got the wolf's eyes too."

He settled back against the tree trunk. "Perhaps it'll be all right."

They stayed there, resting and chatting idly, as the shadows lengthened and the sun settled towards the far edge of the plain, finally lying down around the fire to sleep, covering themselves with the skins.

When Max woke, it was well after dawn and Trudie and Tammi were both up and moving about, each of them teasing him for his indolence. The night had been crisp and cool, but comfortable by comparison with those in the mountains. Trudie unearthed the fire, and they divided the smoked meat between them, eating a little by way of breakfast. They filled the waterskins brim full, each of them taking one. Then, bows ready and most of their clothes in their packs, they set off across the plain.

The soil was dry and peaty, and purple heather grew in profusion, as far as the eye could see. Where they could, they followed animal trails, because the heather, knee high or more, made the going difficult, and was hard on bare legs. The first couple of hours' walking were pleasant, in the cool of the morning, and Trudie and Tammi shot a hare each, up against a low crag. But the day heated up remorselessly as the sun rose higher in the sky. The vegetation and scattered outcrops of rock seemed to throw the heat back up at them, and soon they were all stripped to the waists again, walking mechanically on, pushing through the heather. The only sounds were insects amongst the heather flowers, the sound of it moving past their legs, a curlew somewhere over the moor. Distance blurred into haze, nearer rocks and slopes shimmering in the heat. At length Trudie stopped.

"We'll have to find shelter," she said. "This heat's exhausting, and we'll use all our water."

Max and Tammi nodded.

"Over there?"

A low outcrop of rock rose out of the heather, slightly to the right of their path. Ten minutes' walking found them on it, but the contours were too smooth to offer any shelter. It was another hour before they found a crag steep and tall enough to have a shaded face. They sat down gratefully in its shade, hotter, more tired, and more dehydrated than they had intended. They drank a little water, and settled down to rest in the shade of the rock, until the worst of the day's heat was past. Small green lizards scuttled across the rock, seeking out insects, and a larger snake came silently out to bask in the sun ten yards or so away, watched, wide eyed, by Tammi. The sunlight was blinding on the rock, the heat seeming to press down upon them.

The hours passed. Now and then, one of them would speak, but mostly they sat in silence, eyes half closed, watching the waves of heat shimmering over the heather.

Buzzards rode the air currents high over the moor, against a painfully bright backdrop of blue. As midday wore into afternoon the heat moderated a little as the sun sank in the sky, aided by a slight, hot breeze that had begun to blow. Max got unwillingly to his feet.

"Come on," he said. "We ought to move on."

They walked until the sun was touching the crests of the mountains they had crossed, now miles distant behind them, their lower foothills cloaked in thin haze. Casting long shadows, they stopped by another of the small crags. Max and Trudie gathered old, dead heather, while Tammi skinned and gutted the hares they had shot. They made the fire on the rock itself, afraid that it would spread to the heather of the plain. There was nothing to spit the flesh on, so they sat around the fire, waiting for the flames to die down a little. Above them, the sky was a flawless blue, the colour of starlings' eggs. Max sat, hugging his knees, watching the mist gathering over the moor, the firelight playing on the girls' faces, the shadows thickening against the mountains. Trudie had said little all afternoon, and now seemed preoccupied, turned in on herself. Abruptly, Tammi put her hand on his arm, pointed up at the sky.

"Look," she said.

A silver speck moved across the great bowl of the sky above them, reflecting all the colours of the setting sun, trailing a thin banner of cloud. Stained the colour of the sunset, the trail stretched back as far as the mountains.

"What is it?"

In wonder, he watched the thing moving, watched the trail of cloud springing out of space a little way behind it. As it moved away, arrow straight towards the east, a low rumble ebbed down out of the sky. He watched as the sound faded, realising he had been holding his breath.

"I've never seen anything like that."

"It's still in the sunlight. It must be so high."

He nodded, still watching.

"It looks like metal," Tammi said. "Like the rope clips, when the sun shines."

"Yes," he said, still looking up. "Yes."

Trudie, too, had been watching silently. Now she said:

"I remember once, when I was little, my mother telling me that people from before had things that flew."

"It's going in the same direction as we are."

"Yes." She spoke very quietly, almost to herself. "East."

He looked at her, but she was lost in thought, gazing up at the sky.

They watched as the trail lengthened towards the horizon, growing wider and fainter above their heads. It was almost dark. At last Max roused himself, put the meat into the embers to roast. It was dark when they finished eating, and they lay down by the fire to sleep, drawing their furs over them, their bows within reach.

He woke with a start. It was early dawn, and Trudie was bending over him, gently shaking him awake.

"Max. Max."

"What is it?"

She looked at him, fear minging with resignation in her gaze.

"I told you I would suffer for what I did. I will, today."

He frowned, sitting up.

"What are you talking about?"

"My wolf is dead. Bring your bow. Come and see."

His heart suddenly leaden, he got to his feet, followed her stealthily around the crag, across the heather in the strengthening light. A few hundred yards away there was a second, smaller crag. In amongst some boulders, they found the body of the wolf. Max rolled it over, while Trudie stood

back a little, her face a mask. The animal had bled to death
from an arrow wound in the neck, he saw, its blood pooling
under it. Its body was cold. A second arrow, broken,
protruded from its flank. He hesitated, took hold of the shaft,
worked it out of the wound. Wiping it on the grass, he
inspected it intently, suddenly recognising it for what it was,
sitting back on his heels in shock.

"Oz made this."

She nodded. He looked up at her, his eyes narrowed.

"Why did you kill your wolf?"

"I didn't." He could hardly hear her. "Oz is here,
with Jez White. They've come after me, to kill me."

His mind was racing, assimilating the implications,
one at a time.

"Oz doesn't want to kill you."

"He does. Now."

"I don't understand." He shook his head, as if to
clear it. "They could have tracked us, it's just possible, if
they'd followed us at the time. But they didn't follow us, they
didn't know where to start. We followed no obvious route. It's
impossible that they could have found us here, now."

"Not quite." She spoke almost in a whisper.
"Because I showed them."

"*What*?"

"I put the images in Jez's mind, each night. I showed
him the way we'd gone."

He could not take in what she was saying.

"Why?"

"While I was ill in the shelter," she said. "Perhaps I
was delirious. I dreamed a lot, I had time to think. I thought
about what you'd said, when we were fishing down by the
river, about the people I'd killed, about how part of me
terrified you. I went back to the village, in my mind, I found I
could just do it over that distance. Jez was in the mill, and I
saw into his mind, I saw what finding Orrie, what finding

little Jess, had done to him. I saw the strength and depth of his hatred, and I knew I deserved to die. I thought I owed him that, at least." Her hands were shaking, and a tear ran down her cheek. "That night he had a dream, and when he woke, he knew which way I'd gone."

Woodenly, Max got to his feet. Suddenly he took her in his arms, his head against her shoulder, holding her to him with all his strength.

"Trudie, Trudie," he managed at last, his voice choked. "What have I done, judging you, heaping guilt on you, after what you've had to suffer?"

"Everything you said was true."

"Truth." He shook his head, bitterly. "Perhaps what's true depends on where you're standing." He looked up into her eyes. "You never told me about this, either."

"This is different. I deserved this." She shuddered. "I've told you everything, now. No more deceit, ever. No more games."

He fell silent, then he said:

"This isn't just about what you deserve, whether or not you really do. It's about Tammi and I, who love and need you. That's why Jez would have been better left to sleep, because you can't undo the past, however hard you try. And there are other ways to cope with guilt, apart from even more suffering." He sighed. "I shouldn't have betrayed you, by reacting the way I did."

"I don't want the way I am to change you. I want you to go on doing what you think is right."

"I'm so sorry." He sighed again, picking up his bow. "We ought to get back to Tammi."

They made their way back across the heather, back to the crag, round the rock to where they had spent the night, to be stopped in their tracks by what they saw. The ashes of their fire were there, but Tammi had gone. The water, the skins, the packs, the spare arrows, everything, all gone.

Fourteen

Fear and anger rose up together in Max, the anger directed mainly at himself, that he had been so stupid not to foresee this, the moment that Trudie told him.

She was standing next to him, immobile, her face frozen by shock.

"Quick!" he said to her, taking her hand. "Back the way we came."

He led her round the back of the crag, out of arrow shot, drew her down beside him among the rocks, his mind working furiously.

"They've taken Tammi," she said.

"Wait a minute," he said. "These are, or were, decent men. Tammi hasn't done anything wrong. They won't have killed her, hurt her, certainly not yet. Search for her. Use your mind. You know you can. Go on. Do it."

"They've taken Tammi, to get at me." Her eyes were still vacant with shock.

"Trudie, did you hear me? Do it. Do what I said."

She closed her eyes then, raised her face up to the sunrise. He waited, watching her, holding her hand, the seconds seeming like hours. At last her eyes flickered open.

"She's there," she said, her voice shaky with relief. "They've tied her up, gagged and blindfolded her, but they haven't hurt her. She's terrified."

"Go back," he said. "Go in her mind. Show her we're here, that we know, that it's going to be all right."

She closed her eyes again. He scanned the heather on every side, looking for movement, but there was nothing, only a hare crouching, watching him. Next to him, Trudie opened her eyes.

"I touched her. She knows we know, she's calmer. She's lying in the heather, somewhere over there." She pointed beyond the outcrop.

"Now," he said. "I need to know everything you know. How did they kill the wolf?"

"My courage failed me in the night," she said. "I knew where they were sleeping, and I sent it to kill Jez, for all that I'd shown him the way here, that I knew he deserved to kill me. I couldn't have touched Oz." She looked at him, and the weariness in her eyes appalled him. "But Jez was too good. He'd kept watch, saw it coming, and killed it in time. It was so stupid, so weak of me."

"Can't you kill them both, the way you killed your father?"

She looked shocked.

"I didn't intend to do that to him. I don't know if I could do it again. Even if I could, it might hurt you and Tammi, even kill you. Remember."

He nodded.

"Then can't you get in their minds, like you do with the animals? Force them let her go? Make them go away, or kill each other?"

Again, she looked troubled.

"I've never invaded another person like that. I tried it with a cat once, in the Ruins, and even then it was horrible." She shuddered. "It felt like rape." She looked at him. "I don't know what would happen."

"No." He hesitated. "Have they got dogs?"

"I don't think so. I'd know if they had."

"Right." He paused for a moment. "We need to think. They've got Tammi, all our stuff, all the water. They know where we are. They know you can see what's in my mind, that you can call me. They know that somehow you killed your father, that you can control the wolves. They don't know whether you've got any more wolves. It's you they want, and you they'll be afraid of. Oz knows the way I think, but then I know the way he thinks." He paused. "As for us, we know roughly where they are. We've got our bows and arrows, and we've got you."

She nodded, mutely.

"I'm going to go and try and talk to Oz," he said after a moment. "Try to find out where he's coming from."

"They might kill you."

"They might. But I don't think so. Oz has only ever done good to me, and I to him, so far as I know."

"I'll understand," she said, looking at him, "if you don't come back."

He returned her gaze, slowly shook his head.

"I'm even more certain to come back," he said, "now that they've taken Tammi. They oughtn't to have done that."

"I am so lucky in you, Max. But what I've brought you to."

Again, he hesitated.

"You're what could swing this," he said, half to himself. He turned back to her. "Be in my head when I talk to Oz. See what I see, hear what I hear. In case I miss something."

She nodded.

"If you're sure."

"Go back to the other crag over there, where we found the wolf, and hide in the rocks. Take your bow and arrows. Keep down in the heather. Whatever happens, don't let them know where you are. When you get there, come in my head. Then I'll go out to talk to Oz."

He could see she was near to tears.

"Be careful, Max."

"Go on," he said gently. "Be careful yourself. Remember they'll kill you as soon as look at you."

She went down from the crag in a stooping run, her bow under her arm, and disappeared into the heather. He sat in the rocks and waited, as the deceptive stillness closed in, anxiously looking around him for movement, but there was none. The sun was rising higher in the sky, and the song of a solitary skylark floated down at him out of the blue. He thought of Tammi tied up with her fear, wishing he could go back twenty years and untwist it all, yet knowing that the twist, the pain, was as old as time. At length a gentle touch came in his head, and he knew that she was ready. He fingered his bow, then laid it and his quiver down in the rocks in front of him.

"Oz!" he shouted. "It's me. Max. I know you're out there. I want to talk."

Silence. Only the skylark, and the scratch of a lizard's claws on the rock. He imagined Oz, if he intended to answer at all, moving through the heather, away from Tammi and Jez.

"Oz! It's Max. Answer me! No weapons. I want to talk."

Nothing, but for the skylark. He thought he saw a movement in the heather.

"Oz! I'm going to stand up now. I need to talk to you."

Slowly, he got to his feet, his palms moist, expecting an arrow at any moment, but none came. Suddenly Oz's voice, from somewhere in the heather, so familiar that he had to fight the temptation to walk forward, smiling.

"You know it's her we want, Max."

"She isn't here. I'm on my own."

"Then there's nothing to talk about."

"I need to understand," he said. "Why you're here. We lived under the same roof for years."

Silence, for a moment.

"All right, then." Slowly, the smith stood up, about fifty feet away, spreading empty hands in the same gesture as Max. "Talk costs nothing, and we're long over due for one."

They walked forward towards each other. When they were only feet apart, Max extended his hand, feeling foolish. Oz took it and shook it, gravely.

"No knife."

"No knife."

By mutual consent, they sat down on opposite ends of a boulder.

"Look at the state of you," said Oz after a moment.

Despite himself, Max grinned.

"You aren't a lot better."

"We had a time of it in the mountains. As I expect you did."

Max nodded. After a moment, he said:-

"You've done me nothing but good, Oz. Yet you're here."

"The village is a strange place now, with so many gone."

"You didn't go with the men, when they went out after her."

"No I didn't, and I still don't care too much about what any of them think. But it was you who said to me that we all have to live with ourselves." He paused. "Well, then, this is how it went. When you left I was already wondering if the wolf attacks had anything to do with her, because it all fitted with what you'd told me, and when they stopped after you'd gone, well, it all added up. I could have understood her taking the men, the ones out after her, but not the women and the children. Not Orrie and Jess, Max, for God's sake."

Max sighed.

"I can't justify everything she did. I can just ask you to try and understand."

"I went to see Jez that morning," the smith said. "He was almost mad with grief. I helped him bury Orrie and the little one, behind the mill there. Then, in the next couple of days, he started getting this fixation that he knew where she'd gone, that he could find her. I wondered about that too, knowing what she can do. I spent a couple of days brooding about it all. I thought a lot about her, wondering if she was just playing with Jez, luring him out here for some kind of weird game. I was worried about you, too, what you'd got into. No matter which way I ran it through, I could only get one answer. She has to be killed, before she does this again. She can reach out for anything she wants, Max, if not now then one day, and twist it till it breaks. There's never been anything like her before, I'm sure of that now. So I came with Jez. I reckoned I owed him that." He looked up. "Maybe you can't see it clearly, because you love her. Or maybe she's been in your head and messed with it."

Max felt her making to leave him, then, but he closed his eyes, filled his mind with reassurance, said:

"When you pick up a weapon, even in self defence, sometimes you do wrong. I know she's powerful, maybe even beyond her own imagining. She's more wounded than crazy, and more alone, more hurt, than you or I can ever imagine. She isn't evil, no more than the rest of us, unless having evil done to you makes you evil."

"I won't deny she's never had any sort of a life." The smith sighed. "I'm sorry, Max. It's too late now to worry about what put the twist in her. As long as she lives, no one else, no one at all, is safe. You least of all. I've never been more certain of anything."

Max fell silent, knowing that he had lost, that he had failed in the near impossible task of explaining.

"It's strange," he said at last. "We're both here for the same reasons. Because we care." He looked into the grey eyes. "You were right. There isn't anything to talk about, is there?"

"You mean as much to me as anyone, Max. But you know I'm not going to let you stop this, not now. Don't get between us and her."

"It was a smart move to snatch Tammi," he said. "But can you imagine what she's thinking, expecting now, after what happened to her?"

"We haven't hurt her. We aren't going to."

"Maybe not physically. But use your imagination, Oz."

The smith shrugged.

"I'm sorry, Max. You do what you have to."

Max got to his feet, and Oz said:

"You know I can't let you go back to her."

They stood tensed, feet apart, the boulder between them, eyeing each other warily. Max knew he would never outrun Oz, but Trudie was invisible, hundreds of yards away, and he could see no other option but to try. Abruptly Oz made a grab for his arm, and he moved back, catching his heel on a heather root, cursing. Unable to help himself, he overbalanced, fell backwards. In an instant, Oz was on him, pinioning his arms, grunting as Max kicked at him. Max looked up into his eyes, and suddenly it was as if something stirred in his head, shot out forwards through his forehead. His eyes felt as if they had just stared at the sun. He blinked. Oz had released him, was on his feet, staggering back, holding his head. Understanding broke over Max. He rolled over, sprang to his feet, turned and sprinted back towards the outcrop, crashing through the heather. Once he was among the rocks he dropped to his knees, gathering up his bow and arrows, looked up, cautiously, over the rock. Trudie was gone from his mind, and Oz was sitting on the boulder, his head in his hands. Max took several deep breaths, trying to still his racing heart. After a few moments Oz got to his feet, still rubbing his forehead, his hand over his eyes. Unsteadily, he walked away through the heather, dropping out of sight, after a few moments, into a small defile in the near distance. The sound of the skylark came back.

Max was suddenly conscious of the heat of the sun on his neck. The back of his throat was dry. After a moment he crawled out from the rocks, down the other side of the crag, and into the heather, working his way slowly, on hands and knees, towards the place where the wolf had died. Gently, Trudie touched him again, and he sensed her desire that he stop, watch to his right. Incredibly, without warning, he saw her stand up among the rocks of the crag, in full view, exposed to an arrow shot. He fought the desire to shout, to tell her to get down, to run to her and protect her. To his right, perhaps sixty feet away, Jez Yates's head slowly appeared out of the heather, drawing his bow. Feverishly, Max reached for an arrow, nocked it, shouted at the top of his voice. The sound reached Yates as he released his arrow, and he jumped, the shot going wide. Flashing a glance to his left, he dropped down on his hands and knees, hidden again. Max had had no time to shoot. He dropped down himself, perspiring, listening, straining to hear the slightest sound. He knew she would be angry, and he filled his own mind with anger at her stupidity in taking such risks, in case she was looking. Again, the insects and birdsong came back.

After this, nothing happened for what seemed an age. Trudie remained absent from his mind. He was beginning to suffer from thirst, sprawled in the heather in the full glare of the sun, and, not daring to sit up and take the morning's warmer clothes off, he was losing a lot of water in sweat. He was frequently tempted to move forward and seek out Yates, but knew that the man was probably doing the same as he, and that the one who moved would be at the disadvantage. Or perhaps Yates had pulled back. Suddenly, he felt Trudie in his mind again, and knew she was near him. The heather parted to his left, and she was beside him, her hands and knees grazed from crawling.

"You mustn't expose yourself," he whispered. "They only need one good shot."

"I'm sorry," she replied, her face close to his. "I wanted to draw him. Our only chance is to separate them, get to them one at a time." She closed her eyes for a moment. "One of them always stays with Tammi. I can hear what she hears."

He nodded.

"They'll find it harder to hunt us, then." He paused, shutting his own eyes, opening them again. "What did you do to Oz?"

"I'm sorry. I took a terrible risk, but I knew he'd caught you."

"You didn't hurt me. What happened?"

Her eyes were wide.

"I don't really know. I was in your mind, I knew he'd caught you. Then you looked at each other. It just seemed natural that I might be able to reach him, then. I just reached out for him, but through you, with a fraction of the feeling of when I was with my father, then pushed a little at him, at his awareness." She paused. "It's hard to explain in words. I was worried that I'd harmed you."

"It's all right." He reached out, gently touched a fresh graze on her cheek. "If only we'd explored this. Found out what you can and can't do."

"I can show you what I'm thinking, see what you're thinking. It isn't the same as words. Memories are deeper, different. I haven't really tried."

He nodded.

"I call it the mindsea," she whispered. "I have some idea of where they are in it, in relation to the everyday world. Oz is back with Tammi, nursing a headache, over there. Jez is still in front of us, not far away, listening, not moving. I can see what they see, too, see what they feel, if I'm careful. But if I have to touch them hastily, like just now, then they know. They're on their guard anyway, because they're expecting it, and they're getting more used to how my touch feels, better at recognising it. I'm having to give too much away."

"Can you move, work, in the mindsea and in the everyday?"

"Not really, not at the same time. I have to keep switching."

When he did not reply, she said:

"Tammi's still terrified. She thinks she knows what they'll do to her."

He touched her cheek again in reassurance, and she said:

"I heard what Oz said about me. It's me they want. I know you would look after her for me. Better, in many ways, than I could myself."

He moved his head slightly, kissed her gently, fleetingly, on the forehead.

"You heard what I said to Oz, too. Remember you're all there is, for Tammi as well as me."

She nodded slowly, biting her lip.

"There are two of us," he whispered. "We know roughly where Jez is, but he doesn't know where we are. Oz is still with Tammi, right?"

"Yes."

"You're our real advantage," he said. "Let's each go one side of Jez. Touch me when you think we're level, then stay still. Stay in the mindsea and watch. I'll move towards him, then. Try and watch what he sees and hears, but keep your bow ready. Try to help me if he sees me."

She nodded, turned, crawled stealthily away to his left. Trying to move as silently as he could, he set off himself, the bow under his arm, parting the heather stems with his face. Cobwebs irritated his nose, a wasp buzzed irritatingly around his face. Once he froze, seeing a small snake less than a foot way. Motionless, it regarded him for a long moment, turned, slid noiselessly away. He moved on, holding his body close to the ground. Abruptly, Trudie was in his head, and he knew he had to stop, wait, she was not in position yet. Now, now she was ready. His stomach almost on the ground, he turned left, cursing the tiny sounds which every movement made, moved forward. Looked suddenly into the eyes of Jez Yates, not ten feet away, sitting bent double, holding his bow horizontal, ready drawn. Icy fear filled him, he knew that he was trapped, that he could not move, like the time he confronted the wolf in the village.

Something, fear, doubt, momentarily clouded the man's eyes, then there was a swish and a thud, and he jerked forward, eyes widening in disbelief. He let go the bowstring, and his arrow sang past Max, missing him by inches, so that he felt its wind on his face.

"Oz! Oz!" Yates was shouting. His voice bubbled, blood appeared on his lips.

Another swish and thud, and his head fell forward, an arrow protruding from the base of his skull. He twitched convulsively, but could not make a sound. He rolled to his side and lay still, his fingers slowly relaxing on the bow. Behind him, Trudie stood, twenty feet or so away, a third arrow already on her bow, shock in her eyes.

"You're safe," she said.

His heart pounding, he straightened his arms, sat up, nodded slowly.

"I tried to touch him, stop him moving, but I could feel it slipping. I could see his head. I just had time to stand up, draw the bow. I was afraid of killing you." She walked slowly forward, stood looking down at Yates, tears filling her eyes. "So this is how it ends for him," she said softly, her voice choked with emotion. "Far from home, dead by my hand, I who murdered his family, when he bore me no malice at the start. Worse, when my own guilt brought him here."

Abruptly. she dropped her bow and arrow, stood with clenched fists, her face contorted, her whole body trembling. Wearily, Max got to his feet, pulled her down beside him in the heather, took her in his arms, stroked her cheek, her hair, his gaze fixed on the plain behind her.

"Trudie, Trudie," he whispered. "Not now, not yet. Oz will have heard. Remember he still has Tammi."

Slowly, she quietened, at last turning a tear stained face to him. She sniffed, wiping at the tears with a dirty hand. He held her, wiped the tears from her cheek. Silently, he took Yates's bow and arrows from him, closed his eyes. Then, a little way apart, concentrating intently, they worked their way back to the first crag, crawled to their hiding place among the rocks.

"Go in Tammi's head," said Max. "Show her, reassure her it won't be long."

She closed her eyes, opened them again, moments later, unfocussed, vacant, full of horror, so that Max's belly turned to ice.

"What is it? Trudie, what is it?"

"Oz. He's doing things to her."

He took both her hands, shook them gently, urgently.

"What things? What's he doing?"

"He's taking her clothes off. She's still tied up, still gagged, blindfolded." Trudie's voice was very quiet, dead, absolutely empty of emotion. "He's touching her, stroking her leg. She wants to scream, but she can't." A tear ran from each of her eyes. "He understands me too well." She got to her feet. "I'll end it, Max. I'll go to him now."

Max stood too, still holding both her hands, blazing fury rising within him. So this was to be the way.

"Which way?" he said urgently. "Which way are they, Trudie?"

Distracted, she pointed.

"Over there. Let me go now, Max. Let me go to her."

He released her hands, scooped up his bow and quiver, stood looking, for a long moment, in the direction in which she had pointed. She began to walk, numbly, empty handed, out across the heather, oblivious of him, oblivious of everything. Max lowered his head and sprinted, off to her right, towards a small rock outcrop lying beyond the small defile down which Oz had walked. He couldn't see straight, his heart pounded in his ears. He crashed down the defile, across a small depression. They weren't here. Moments later, he came to the crag, ran round the back of it, dropped onto hands and knees as he came to a crest, wiping sweat from his eyes. It was no use, he could only see heather. Where were they? If Oz has left Tammi, is holding his bow, he thought, Trudie is dead already. He scrambled down the crag, losing his footing, falling, rolling, uncaring of the rocks. Dropping the bow, wasting precious seconds picking it up again. Running forward, coming to another defile, a dry watercourse with a grassy bottom, suddenly stopping in his tracks.

Tammi lay tied up on the grass at the foot of the slope, immobile, naked, her knees drawn up under her chin, her body quivering. Oz kneeled next to her, a hand on her leg, a knife held at her neck.

"Don't bother trying anything, Max," he said quietly, not turning round. "No sense in this one dying."

At the top of the opposite slope, Trudie paused.

"I'm here," she said, in the same dead voice. "Please leave her alone now."

Oz looked up.

"God forgive me," he said, "but I had to finish this, and finish it I will. Come down here, beside her."

Woodenly, Trudie began to descend the slope. Intently, moving very slowly, Max reached back, slid an arrow out of his quiver, fitted it to the bow. Drew it back, eyes narrowed, as Trudie came down beside her sister, knelt on the ground, tears spilling down her cheeks. Closed his eyes, opened them, then released the bowstring.

Inches from Tammi's throat, the arrow took Oz in his knife hand, flinging it back, the knife spinning away into the grass. Instantly, Trudie sprang to her feet, leaping at Oz, battering at his face with both her fists. He flailed at her with his uninjured arm, striking her on the cheek. She staggered back, her foot catching Tammi's leg, falling backwards, as Max's second arrow took Oz in the back. The smith staggered, looking up at him in amazement, then reached round, his face contorted, and wrenched the arrow free, holding it in both hands, standing over Trudie where she lay, wide eyed, on her back. Frantically, Max nocked another arrow, drew the bow. The bolt struck Oz in the neck, and his whole body jerked, then sagged. The arrow fell from his nerveless fingers, and he dropped forwards, half across Trudie, his face working. As she struggled out from under him, Max was already beside Tammi, cutting at her bonds, then her gag, with his knife. Wordlessly, blindly, the three of them clung to each other, shaking with sobs, on the grass next to the smith's body.

Fifteen

Trudie woke in the early dawn of the next morning, after a night of fitful, broken sleep, worsened by the fact that each of them now had to watch through part of the night, in case wild animals came. There seemed little to wake for, any more, but she rolled over, sat up in the soft light, the fur she lay under damp with dew, rubbing her eyes. To find that she and Tammi were alone, that Max had gone. She got to her feet, ignoring cramped limbs, intently scanning the plain around her in every direction. Then she closed her eyes, held her face up to the sky, relaxing, breathing slowly. After a few moments her eyes opened, and she shook her head slightly, tenderness and concern on her face. She bent and picked up her bow and arrows, looked quickly back at Tammi, still asleep beside the ashes of the fire, and set off across the heather.

After a few minutes' walking she came to the defile where it had ended the previous day. She hesitated for a moment on its rim, looking down. All that remained, even after so little time, were some flattened grass, and two dark patches of blood.

She looked across the defile to the small crag. Max was sitting on the rock, sphinx like, absolutely immobile, beside the pile of rocks under which they had buried Oz the previous afternoon. His hands were clasped in his lap, his bow at his side, as he sat gazing out sightlessly across the plain, towards where the sun would rise. Her heart went out to him, and she walked quietly over to the crag, climbed the rock, sat down silently beside him. Hesitantly, after a moment, she reached out and took one of his hands between both of hers, saying nothing. The look in his eyes was the look that had been in Tammi's when they had started this journey, and her eyes pricked with tears.

They sat there for a long time, next to each other, as the sky brightened in the east and the first birds took wing. Yesterday still burned in her mind, her thoughts revolving in destructive loops of guilt and regret. They had done nothing after it ended, resting exhausted in the shelter of the crag during the heat of the day, clinging to each other at first, then later sitting against the rock, each of them holding one of Tammi's hands. To Trudie's immense relief, Tammi had come out of her shock after some hours, holding Max's hands in hers, telling him again and again that now, a second time, he had saved her, given her the hope to go on. But he had made no response, walled off from her by his grief, and Trudie had turned away, unable to confront this, this last thing that she had done. At last, as the afternoon drew on and the day cooled, Max had got to his feet, gone down to the defile, to Oz's body. Slowly, methodically, he had removed his arrows, cleaned them as best as he could. There was no way that they could bury Oz, but the girls had come down then, helped Max drag the body up under the crag, where they had covered it in loose stones, heaping them up until they had used everything that was small enough to move. Max had sat down beside the stones, uncommunicating, unseeing. Tammi had taken her bow and had gone out onto the moor to hunt, and Trudie had stayed near Max, sitting silently on the crag a little distance away, watching the sun set behind the mountains. When, as night thickened over the plain, she had taken his hand, led him over to the fire Tammi had made at their original sleeping place, he had not resisted, allowed himself to be led.

Now, as the sun rose over the plain, she closed her eyes, touched her sister's mind now that she had woken, over by the other crag, soothing her until the morning sickness was past, showing her where she was herself. Then she withdrew, coming back to the everyday, knowing that Tammi would start a fire, cook the hare she had surprised the previous evening. Beside her, Max stirred.

"I've killed the only person who ever showed me kindness," he said, very quietly. "The only person who mattered to me in the world, other than you and Tammi."

"I brought you to this."

"No," he said slowly, shaking his head. "I saw you, I saw the way you are, and then I chose this."

"Oz thought I'd messed with your head."

"No." Again he shook his head, gazing into the sunrise, his face stained like copper. "You never meant to. You were only ever you. It was my choice to be here."

She made no reply, and he said:

"He didn't think I'd do it. I saw it in his eyes after I shot him. He was so sure he was right that he still thought I'd see it his way." He hesitated, then went on: "You said he understood you, but he didn't. He only understood you enough to hurt you, just like all the others. He had no idea why I love you."

She tightened her grip on his hand.

"Perhaps he was right," she said. "I only ever hurt the people I love. Perhaps your first arrow should have been for me. One for me, one for Tammi. To end all this pain."

"No. To use Tammi to get to you was wrong. More wrong, in a strange way, perhaps, than anything else that has been done. You know, and he knew, that that was why I killed him."

They sat next to each other, watching the sunrise.

"You, me, Oz," he said at last. "All trying to do what they thought was right."

"Yes."

He turned to her.

"What will you do, Trudie, with this seeing?"

"Try to share it with Tammi and you. No more games, no more deceit." She looked at him, and yet again he saw the despair in her eyes. "I've been so long alone that I was too afraid to share, to trust, and so I've killed Oz and Jez. Orrie, little Jess, all the others."

"Trust me, from now on," he said softly. "I'll try not to ask too much more."

Silently, they embraced. At last Max got to his feet, stood for a long time in silence, looking at Oz's grave. Then he took Trudie's hand, and they walked slowly away through the heather, to where a thin smudge of smoke marked the position of Tammi's fire.

She had cooked the hare, and after they had shared it they took stock of what they had. No food, five bows and five remaining quivers of arrows. All their own equipment, what little Oz and Jez had been carrying. Their own water skins had been cut, but Oz and Jez had had two, each still about half full. They sat around the dying fire, looking at each other.

"Do you think we should go back to the mountains for water?" Trudie asked.

Max shook his head, and so did Tammi.

"I never want to see this place again."

"Neither do I."

Trudie looked at each of them in turn.

"Perhaps we'll be lucky, and find water."

"There was a moon last night," Max said. "Almost full. The nights are quite cold. If we travel early morning, late evening, and at night when the moon's up, we'll cover ground more quickly, and need less water."

The girls nodded assent. Minutes later, packs and bows on their backs, they moved off, towards the rising sun.

In the near distance a low ridge rose against the sky, covered in what seemed to be short yellow grass. In another hour they were on its flanks. The air was almost windless, the day already becoming hot. They had tied their lightest, thinnest clothing to their heads, to protect their heads, necks, and shoulders from the worst of the sun. Filthy, half naked, they stood next to each other on the low ridge, hands held up to shield their eyes, gazing with narrowed eyes out across the plain. The distant hills, the ones they had seen from the mountains, shimmered in the heat, more illusion than real.

"It looks so dry."

Trudie nodded, worry deepening the lines around her eyes.

"Yes."

Thin grass and sedge now covered the ground, and the soil was sandy, gravelly. Low crags still outcropped at intervals, with occasional boulder fields and scattered rocks.

"We should shelter soon."

"Yes. But where?"

They moved out across the flats. Again, the first two crags offered no shade. A boulder field ran away from the second, towards the northeast, and reluctantly they settled down in the scant shade offered by the largest rocks. It proved a poor choice, as the day wore on. The rocks trapped the heat, and the still air between them became unbearable, like a furnace. As the sun rose towards the zenith, the shade decreased to narrow strips, barely wide enough to huddle in, so that arms and legs suffered from sunburn. It was too hot to catch the lizards that scuttled across the rock, despite the first stirrings of hunger. They barely moistened their lips with water, but by the time the sun dropped towards the mountains, and the pastels of evening began softening the rocks, their throats were dry, and one of the water skins was empty.

They emerged from the rocks to find the air cooling at last, the faintest of breezes stirring in the wiry grass. Setting out into the east, towards the mockingly distant hills, they managed a good three hours' walking before it became too dark to continue. There was nothing substantial enough to use for a fire, so they settled down together to sleep, backs against a rock, with Max taking the watch until the moon rose.

His hoarse shout woke the girls. Sitting up with a start, scrabbling for their bows, they saw the silhouettes of a pack of wild dogs, their eyes reflecting the light of the newly rising moon. For some moments the air was alive with the swish of arrows, with snarls and yelps. The plain grew still once more. As the moon rose they saw that three of the animals lay dead. They must have wounded others, but they had escaped, with arrows still in them. They took the arrows from the carcasses, recovered a few more from amongst the grass, but it was a near hopeless task in the moonlight. Reckoning up, they found that they had lost almost half their arrows.

The heat of the previous day had dissipated quickly, and the air was now cool. They spent precious time getting what they could from the bodies of the dogs. Working with difficulty in the light of the rising moon, they cut the hearts out of the animals, taking one each, squeezing the blood out into their mouths. It seemed wasteful to leave so much meat, but it was water they really needed, and their packs were more valuable. In the end Max cut out the livers, tying them to his belt, and they dismembered two of the bodies, Trudie and Tammi carrying two haunches each. They set off again across the plain, leaving the north star to their left.

Under the staring eye of the full moon, the plain had the quality of dream. Distance had little meaning, the ground, rocks, and crags appearing ghostlike in the silver light. Rocks that appeared nearby would keep receding as they walked, in reality distant. The sounds made by their feet on the ground, on loose rocks, seemed unnaturally loud. After the encounter with the dogs, all three of them walked warily, with arrows ready in their bows, intently scanning the shadows. In the event they saw no other animals all night.

Covering the flat ground in the moonlight proved surprisingly easy, difficulties only arising if obstacles were hidden in the shadows of larger rocks. The sky was an immense arch over their heads, alive with stars. Once, looking up, Max saw a shower of meteors dart across it, each dying into oblivion as it went. They came on no water, running or standing, all night.

As dawn strengthened in the east, the hills they were making for were nearer, but still distant in haze. Their legs tired now, eyes heavy from lack of sleep, they stopped on the wiry grass to rest. Max cut some of the dog liver into strips, and they chewed that, carefully inspecting it for worms. They each took a little water. The second skin was now less than a quarter full. Before the sun rose, they were on their way again, Max in particular flagging a little now. Though his legs were stronger after the days of travelling, he was still at a disadvantage by comparison with the girls.

Talking about it afterwards, all three of them could remember little of the remainder of the journey across the plain. The grassland was devoid of rocks now, and they could find no shelter all day, having little option but to continue walking, as the ground was as hot as the air. The water was soon gone, and exhaustion forced frequent stops, as by now they had been walking for almost eighteen hours. They ate the rest of the liver, chewed the dog meat for the moisture it contained, but it offered little solace, even the larger pieces drying rapidly in the heat. The rest of the day, the following night, the next morning, were a nightmare of thirst, their throats parched, tongues swollen, lips cracked. The hills, nearer all the time, shimmered mockingly in the heat, their slopes impossibly green, blanketed in forest. Everything danced in the heat, reality assuming the quality of hallucination, fuelled by dehydration and lack of sleep.

Trudie remembered the most about that last morning. The hills seemed close enough to touch now, and the going was becoming rougher, the ground more broken. She remembered labouring up a low ridge, slipping backwards on loose gravel, almost as far as she progressed at each step. Biting her lip until the blood came, she forced herself on. Her feet hurt at every step, she seemed to have lost her boots. Her face, lips, shoulders, arms and legs, were peeling, raw with sunburn. A little way behind her, Tammi fell to her hands and knees, vomited again, a thin, empty sound. It was too late for her morning sickness, perhaps the last of the dog meat had gone bad. She knew she ought to go to Tammi, help her, but she had no energy, could not climb this slope again a second time. Standing unsteadily atop the ridge, the air seemed cooler, and, impossibly, she thought that it smelled of moisture, of woodland.

Behind her, Tammi was climbing up the stones again, like an animal, on all fours. Trudie could hear her whimpering, then she paused, vomited again. Her face a mask of concentration, she gained the top of the ridge. Her eyes were huge in her burnt, dirt stained face, her hair matted, bleached almost white by the sun. She reached out for her sister's hand, got painfully to her feet.

"Max," she said, trying to moisten her parched lips, her voice no more than a croak. "Max is gone." She looked up at Trudie, her eyes pleading. "Help me find him."

Trudie closed her eyes, opened them again. Unsteadily, she turned, looked back across the low ridges they had been crossing, towards the blazing heat of the plain. She thought she could see something lying there, half way down the last ridge. She blinked. She and Tammi put down the few things they still carried, started down the slope again, walking drunkenly, steadying each other.

After what seemed an age they crossed the dry valley, came to him, lying face down in the grass. He moaned slightly, moved when they bent and touched him. They rolled him over, and he opened his eyes, slitted against the brilliance of the sun. They helped him sit up, but he could not stand, and, even together, lifting him was beyond them. Trudie wanted to cry with the hopelessness, because she knew what this meant, but no tears would come. Nothing was left at all. She and Tammi kneeled in front of him, desperation in their eyes.

"Max," Trudie whispered. "Crawl."

He dropped forwards onto his hands, started to crawl. She and Tammi walked beside him, holding each other. It must have taken him an hour to cross to the opposite slope. The girls forgot their own condition, watching him, feeling every faltering step, but powerless to help. Somehow, between them, they eventually got him up the slope, crawling behind him, pushing him, forcing him to go on, not allowing him to give up, to sleep.

Descending the other side was a little easier, and, as the ground levelled, the grass seemed richer, greener. Perhaps a hundred yards away, Trudie thought she saw a grove of low trees, a small stream running out from between them, losing itself in the sand between there and here, disappearing into the ground. Straightening up, she walked forward, unsteadily. Surely she could hear water now, trickling over rocks? Finer grass grew under her feet now, leaves closed over her head. She fell forward on the cool grass, her face in the water, impossible water, sucking it in, splashing it over her face, hair, shoulders. Rolling over, she sat up, taking the empty water skin from her belt, filling it. Forcing herself to her feet again, she walked back to where Tammi knelt, an arm round Max's shoulders. She poured a little water into her sister's mouth, then into Max's, watching the eyes close in weariness, in thankfulness. Minutes later they were together, in the shade of the nearest tree, and she knew that, at last, it was safe to close her eyes.

They must have slept for the remainder of that day, all of the following night, mercifully undisturbed by any large animals. When Trudie woke, the sun was high in the sky, and she felt at peace, but still very weak. The others were still asleep. She sat up painfully in the dappled shade of the birch grove. The sky was clear, pale blue, seen through the fine leaves. Yards away on the grass, rabbits were feeding. She looked around for her bow, saw that she had nothing, nothing but the few clothes she had slept in. Suddenly cold, she drew the thin fabric about her breasts, trying to remember. Max had almost died. She and Tammi could hardly walk. Her feet hurt. She drew up her legs, looking. Blisters had burst, and the raw flesh was full of dirt, bloody in places.

Slowly, painfully, she got to her feet, almost crying out as the weight came on them. Easing stiffness from her limbs, suddenly very hungry, she turned back in the direction from which they had come. She hobbled slowly across the grassy meadow where the stream ended, climbed the ridge, her face drawn, looking around as she went. There. Full of relief, she picked up her and Tammi's bows, two quivers, her and Tammi's packs, though there seemed little left in either by way of clothes. She could not remember what had happened to the things.

She came down the slope, slowly back across the meadow, sat down at the base of a tree, an arrow nocked on the bow, settling into stillness. After some time, an incautious rabbit ventured out onto the meadow again. Her first arrow found it, and she limped over to get it, a look of satisfaction on her face. It wasn't much, but it would do to start with, with their stomachs so empty. She gathered some sticks and larger branches, rummaged in her pack, sighing thankfully when she saw she still had her tinder box. The fire was burning, and she was sitting with her feet in the stream, trying to clean her wounds, by the time Tammi awoke.

Trudie still had some of her healing herbs, and bound up her injured feet with these, using strips torn from her clothes and soaked in the stream. Tammi could not remember the previous day at all, but Trudie described to her the path they had followed with Max, sent her out to retrace it. She came back with Max's bow and arrows, and another depleted pack. In the afternoon, feeling stronger after eating her share of the rabbit, Tammi went out into the forest with her bow, returning with another rabbit and two doves, having lost only one arrow. Trudie skinned and gutted the rabbit, scraping the two skins clean with her knife. She hung them up to dry, hoping to make moccasins to protect her feet.

The sisters sat in the shade by the stream, watching the water running, the embers of the fire smoking, looking at each other. Their skin was peeling all over their bodies, faces, shoulders, breasts, arms, legs, and their lips were painfully cracked. Their hair was matted, filthy, bleached by the sun. With lingering regret, they took their knives and cropped each other's hair, leaving them both with little more than an inch of ash-blonde stubble. They laughed quietly at each other, anticipating Max's reaction when he woke.

Afternoon was cooling into evening by the time he regained consciousness. At first he looked at Tammi and Trudie with alarm, unable to come to terms with the startling change in their appearances. He was still very weak. He took some water and a little roasted rabbit flesh, and was asleep again well before evening. The girls sat by the fire until nightfall, resting in the shade, chatting idly. This time they divided the night between them, one staying awake to watch.

Max woke not long after the girls next morning. Though still weak, he was alert once more, sitting against a birch trunk talking to Trudie, while she started the fire, and Tammi hunted for doves around the crags in the forest. He kept pausing, looking at her, and she shook her head, laughing at him.

"You look so strange with your hair cut short," he said. "It's been long ever since you were little, as long as I can remember."

"It was almost worth it, just to see your face. Especially yesterday."

"It wasn't very thoughtful of you. The shock might have killed me." He went on looking critically at her, scantily clad as she was. "I can see all your bones."

She giggled.

"You're no picture yourself."

"I don't expect I am." He rolled over. "How are your feet?"

"Better. At least they're more or less clean."

Tammi came back then, with two more doves. After they had cooked and eaten them Max and Tammi settled down in the shade of the birches, and Trudie stitched the rabbit skins into moccasins, sewing them with some gut that she had saved. They rested in the birch grove for the whole of this second day, Max sharing the watches with the girls once the night came.

The next morning they cooked the last two doves, then stamped out the fire's embers and set off into the hills. Max still lacked energy, and Trudie's feet, though far better, were still painful, so they maintained an easy pace, stopping frequently to rest. The hills were gentle and rolling, heavily forested, mainly oak, ash, and the occasional larch. The sun shone from a cloudless sky, and the forest was alive with birdsong. Coming to terms slowly with the renewed abundance of food, they kept their bows ready but did not hunt; there was little point in carrying meat when it could be caught later in the day.

During the afternoon the ground became more hilly, with crags of a fine grained, grey rock outcropping between the trees. Trudie's feet were tender and Max was already tired, so they stopped in the middle of the afternoon. The crags

were honeycombed with caves, many offering ideal
sanctuaries for the night, apparently unoccupied by animal
inhabitants. Insisting that Trudie sit down to rest her feet,
Tammi went off along the line of crags with her bow, while
Max slowly collected wood for a fire. Coming back through
the trees, his arms full of sticks, he watched her sitting on the
flat rock before the cave, running her hands through what
remained of her hair, her eyes closed, face held up to the sun.
After a moment she opened them, smiled.

"No point in hiding, Max. I know you're there."

He came slowly up the gentle slope, put the wood
down beside her.

"You looked at peace," he said. "At last."

She sighed.

"I can't undo the past. But perhaps, at last, there's
hope for a future."

He nodded.

"And the winter, and Tammi's child."

"It'll be all right," she said, suddenly positive.
"Believe it. You'll see."

He smiled, half to himself.

"I used to dream of this, you know. Being alone in
the forest, with you."

"How things change." Her gaze was transparent.

"Some things. But I am as I am."

"I wouldn't be with anyone else. You know that."

"No." He shook his head, angrily because that was
easier than frustration, easier than despair. "Your father once
said I'm not even a man, and he was right. You and Tammi
are beautiful. You deserve better than empty years in the
forest with me."

She reached out to him, taking his hands, drawing
him down on the rock beside her.

"You as you are, and I as I am," she said, very softly.
"I may look all right to you on the outside. I've only ever been

forced, only ever been with my father. I think that, inside, I'm less complete than you." She took him in her arms, drawing him to her, seeing the pain on his face. "What could anyone else offer me, that you haven't? You're teaching me how to love."

"No one had to teach you that. Ask Tammi."

"I know, but she was different, because she depended on me. When you're hurt, you learn to use weapons, to build walls. I know how good I got at that. But what you're giving me is courage." She smiled down at him, cradling his head against her. "Courage to believe in myself, to dare, bit by bit, to give myself away." She held him gently. "The hardest thing of all. Remember, Max, I chose to be with you as much as you with me. That much, at least, is even between us."

Sixteen

The weather changed that night, and next day dawned dull and grey, with a blustery wind lifting the leaves of the trees, driving heavy cloud over the hills. They ate the remains of the doves which Tammi had shot amongst the crags, and set off again through the forest.

The ground rose for perhaps a mile, then sloped away equally gently. They came down to a small stream, where ash trees were scattered in among the oak, and tall plants with bell-like flowers grew in clearer spaces between them. Trudie shivered in the wind, regretting the loss of clothes and furs out on the plain, and Max noticed, meeting her eyes for a moment, taking her hand. Beyond the stream, the trees were larger, and they passed through a grove of tall beeches, their leaves whispering. The ground under the trees was open, covered only in last year's leaves, and Tammi kicked them as she walked, watching them whirl in the air. Then the ground fell away again, oak and sycamore starting to appear, and they crossed another stream, pausing to drink. Trudie leaned against a tree trunk, taking the weight off each of her feet in turn.

At the top of the far slope the ground levelled off again; once more the trees were larger, more widely spaced. Ahead, a bank ran across the slope at right angles to their path. Max frowned. It seemed too regular, too straight, to be natural, but it stretched away between the trees to right and left, as far as the eye could see, unlike anything he had ever seen.

They came up to the bank in minutes. It was more like a wall, perhaps three feet wide by five high, covered with moss, overgrown with plants, with a thinner strip set into the top. A second, identical wall ran exactly parallel to the first, perhaps fifteen feet beyond it. Gingerly, Max touched it.

Scraping it with the end of his bow, he saw that the top strip was metal, untarnished by time. The bulk of the wall reminded him of the material used to build the streets in the Ruins.

"This must be from before," he said hesitantly.

He looked to right and to left. The walls ran straight through the forest as far as they could see to their left, while on the right they curved gently towards the north. Tammi scraped at the metal with her own bow.

"What could it be for?"

"Like all those things in the Ruins," said Max. "Lost to us."

Abruptly, distantly, a low drone came to them, coming and going on the wind, carried from the direction in which they were travelling. Overlaid by a regular low pitched thumping, it seemed to move across their path. They stood still, intent, listening. Max looked anxiously at Trudie.

"What's that?"

She shook her head, still listening.

"I've never heard anything like it."

Slowly the sound grew fainter. They stood still for a minute or two, their heads cocked, listening, but it had faded, did not return. Rousing herself, Trudie climbed over the two parallel walls with difficulty, aided by a fallen tree, and Tammi and Max followed. Beyond, the ground sloped away gently, and they caught a glimpse of water between the trees. Descending the slope, they found themselves on the shore of a large lake. At least a mile wide, it stretched out as far as they could see to left and right, its ends hidden by the forest. Looking along the lake shore, Max wondered how long it would be before they saw the first shadings of autumn in the woods. He could feel rain in the wind, and further down the lake a squall blotted out the more distant forest. He stood for some time, scanning the far shore intently, but could see nothing untoward, no source for the strange sound.

The rain gradually became heavier and colder, sounding on the leaves, beginning to penetrate to the forest floor. They stood, watching the patterns the raindrops made on the waters of the lake, heavier drops beginning to fall on them. Tammi shivered, brushing the wetness from her hair. The narrow shingle beach became rocky to their left, offering shelter of a sort. They huddled on loose stones between some boulders, trying to keep out of the rain, pulling their inadequate clothing round them, watching the wind drive the wavelets, in unending succession, onto the shingle shore.

"We could stay in a place like this," Tammi said suddenly, "if we could build a house, or a big enough shelter."

"Perhaps." Max nodded slowly. "There'd be fish all the year round, even if the hunting was harder in the winter." He hesitated. "Winter clothes would be easy enough. You'd have to build strongly. You'd need a store of dry wood, the winters are probably even colder than where we used to live. But we haven't got proper tools for working wood. I did think of that, before coming away, but I couldn't carry everything."

Trudie sighed.

"Life hangs by a thread."

"I know. And Tammi will be heavy with her child by spring."

The three of them looked at each other.

"It's so hard to think far enough ahead."

"Yes." Max gazed out over the lake. "If we still had the Ruins, or a village to trade with, we'd manage. But by yourself, you can only do so much. There's things like arrow heads." He looked back at the girls. "Perhaps we should stop here for a few days, at least. The fishing and hunting should be good. We can explore round here. Maybe there are caves. Maybe this is where we ought to stay."

Trudie nodded.

"Yes. We're worn out from travelling." She shivered again. "And we need animal skins, to do something about our clothes."

They spent the afternoon gathering wood for a wood pile, and building a shelter down by the lake side, similar to the one Max and Tammi had made when Trudie had the fever, before they crossed the mountains. By early evening the wind had died to a gentle breeze, and the clouds were starting to break up, the sunlight striking through its cover in places, out to the west. They went out hunting together, up the shore of the lake towards the north. After a mile or two they came on a herd of roe deer, grazing in open woodland by the lakeside, fortunately up wind of them. Trudie nocked an arrow and dropped down behind a tree, waiting, while Max and Tammi began to work their way through the forest, keeping the animals between them and the lake. Tammi hid herself after a little time, and Max continued round towards the north. Before he reached the lakeside again the animals had wind of him, and were becoming restive. Hoping that they would not break to the north, he ran towards the herd, shouting, crashing through the undergrowth. They wheeled, turned and ran south east, straight towards Tammi's hiding place. By the time he and Trudie reached her, she had killed a mature doe, to her immense delight, though it had taken three arrows to bring it down.

They tied the deer's legs to a fallen branch, and managed to carry it back to the shelter between the three of them, resting frequently. Trudie started a fire with the drier, smaller wood, and they cooked and ate the heart and liver, leaving the rest of the butchery until the morning. As night thickened over the lake, they walked the few yards down to the shore, sitting together on a rock by the lakeside. They sat gazing out over the almost mirror smooth water, darkening like velvet against the trees on the far shore, watching the fish rising. Trudie sat with her chin on her knees, hugging her legs.

"There's so much food here," she said.

"For now."

"It might still be all right in the winter."

"It might." Next to her, Max shifted. "I wonder if this lake freezes."

"You can fish through ice."

"Yes. But it's difficult and dangerous."

Silence fell between them, then abruptly Tammi put her hand on Trudie's arm.

"Look," she said. "Across the lake." She pointed. "There, where the trees are thinner."

They strained their eyes to see in the deepening gloom.

"A person," Trudie said at last. "In a canoe."

They looked at each other.

"I wonder if he saw our fire." She flashed a glance at Max. "Or she."

They watched the distant figure paddling on, parallel to the far shore.

"He isn't acting interested," said Max after a time.

"Or trying to hide from us," Tammi put in.

"No."

Max sat in silence, thinking. It had crossed his mind that possibly, just possibly, they would encounter other people. They had had no way of knowing what to expect, out here. The three of them had not talked about it, but he knew that how it went, if they met people, would hang on their attitude to a dwarf and two attractive girls, travelling alone. Recalling the encounter in the Ruins, he said nothing, but his eyes met Trudie's, and when she touched his mind, he knew that she was thinking the same.

"I think we should go down the lake to the south in the morning," she said at length. "See what we can find out about them, before we give ourselves away. What they're like, how many of them there are. If we can find them at all. That could have been a solitary traveller or hunter."

Max nodded.

"Yes. Then we can decide whether to go to them. Or maybe trade with them, later. Or move on, so they never know we were here."

It was almost dark, so they went back to the shelter and lay down to sleep, Trudie sitting up to keep watch in case scavengers came to the deer's carcass. Max lay awake for hours in the unaccustomed comfort of the shelter, his mind futilely weighing possibilities, while Tammi slept beside him, and Trudie moved occasionally outside. When she woke him for his watch, he felt that he had never been asleep. Nothing came near them while he watched, looking at the stars shining between the leaves, at their reflection in the lake. He waited until the first stirrings of dawn were showing in the east before he roused Tammi for the last watch, and strangely, then, sleep came almost at once.

When he woke again it was to a morning of utter clarity, the waters of the lake like a mirror, reflecting every colour of the sunrise. He sat up quietly, looking at Trudie asleep beside him, looking at her face as she breathed gently. In the exquisite light it seemed to him unlined, at peace at last. He thought of the morning she had come to him in the smithy, how she had said that she did not want to wake him, and he thought about courage and trust.

Outside, Tammi was asleep too, her back against the shelter, her sleeping face elfin under the rough crop of her hair. He watched her for a moment too, then he smiled, wishing that he had the strength to drag the deer carcass out of sight before waking her. In the end he settled for tickling her face with a grass stem, amusing himself at her expense with a series of remarks about wild animals and how dangerous the forest could be when no one kept watch at night. He desisted, laughing, once she was blushing to her roots, glad that this morning she did not appear troubled by sickness.

He made a small fire with their driest wood, and cooked a little of the flesh from the hindquarters of the deer, trying to keep the smoke to a minimum. Tammi had gone down to the water to fish, and almost at once caught a fine lake trout, over two feet in length. Minutes later she was taken by surprise by the strength of a pull on her line. It cut into her hand, making her cry out, and within seconds she had lost the line and hook. Max got up from the fire and went over to reassure her, saying that it had probably been a pike.

Within an hour they were moving off parallel to the lake shore towards the south, trying to remain in the forest for cover. They could do little to preserve the deer carcass now that their priorities had shifted, but the waste of it irritated Max, especially after their recent privations. Tammi had hung up her fish in the shelter, and they had risked taking nothing with them but weapons and a little cooked venison, left over from breakfast. It was a pleasure to be able to move more easily through the forest, though they took care to cover their tracks in case the shelter should be discovered in their absence.

It took them less than two hours to reach the southern end of the lake. During all that time they had been vigilantly scanning the water and the shores, but had seen nothing but a rich diversity of animal life. The trees grew rooted in peat here, right up against the shore or even in the water, and the ground became marshy, slowing their progress, as they worked their way along the southern shore. Max eyed an osprey's nest in a dead tree, thinking of the size of the eggs, but was deterred by the look in the parent bird's eye. They forded a stream, emerging into more open woodland on its other side, turning north again along the lake's eastern shore. A wide animal trail ran through the trees, and as they came to it Trudie, who was leading, stopped suddenly.

"Look," she said, pointing at the ground.

They looked at the tracks, where a wet flush had left the soil soft.

"Wheel marks," Max said hesitantly. "Narrow, with round edges, and a weird pattern on them. Two wheels that keep crossing each other."

"Yes." Trudie was gazing intently at the marks. "Quite fresh."

They looked at each other.

"We should get off the trail," said Max. "Try to stay concealed."

Trudie nodded abstractedly, closing her eyes, turning her face up to the sun. Moments later her eyes opened again, wide with amazement.

"People," she said breathlessly. "Quite a lot of people. Over there."

She pointed down the trail, where it disappeared over a slight rise. Sunlight was bright between the trees there, as if the forest gave way to a clearing or open meadow.

"They're like us," she went on excitedly. "But their thoughts are all strange. Their minds are full of things I don't understand."

"What sort of things?" Max spoke urgently. "How are they strange?"

"I told you, I can't understand." Again, she slipped into the mindsea, her eyes flicking open after a minute or so. She had paled, and her hands began to quiver. Concern deepening on his face, Max put an arm round her.

"Trudie, what's wrong?"

"I touched one, a young woman, and looked," she said, her eyes huge. "Everything's different, everything's strange."

"How?"

She shook her head, dazedly.

"Everything is brightly coloured. Their eyes reflect like water. There's something as big as a house, made of metal."

He put his arm round her waist, began to lead her off the trail towards some dense undergrowth.

"This needs time. We must find somewhere safe."

"Max. Trudie."

Tammi was staring fixedly down the trail, her bow in her hand.

"Something's coming," she said.

"Run!" Max called, trying to attract her attention, yet not call too loudly. "Tammi! Over here! Over here with us!"

He hesitated, in an agony of indecision as to whether to go back to her, or get Trudie, still slightly shocked, into cover. They were about ten yards from Tammi, partly concealed by undergrowth, when the man came over the rise. Tammi stood frozen, an arrow on her bow, in the middle of the trail.

He was moving faster than anyone could run, sitting on something that shone like metal. He leaned forward on it, moving his feet, concentrating intently on the trail. His arms and legs were bare, his body clad in coloured, tightly fitting clothes. Dark patches covered his eyes, and his head was swollen and shining. Tammi stood absolutely transfixed, unable to move, watching him. Suddenly he must have seen her, because he squeezed with his hands, slewed sideways, coming to an abrupt stop perhaps twenty feet from her. For an instant the silence was absolute. Then he moved a hand slightly, and Tammi raised her bow. The man spoke.

"Don't shoot me!" he said. "I won't harm you."

The words sounded strange, but the language was recognisably the same as their own. Then Trudie must have stepped on a twig, and the man's head snapped round at the sound, seeing movement in the undergrowth. Slowly, still half paralysed by amazement, hardly knowing what she was doing, Tammi began to draw her bow. The man's hand went to something on his belt, brought up a short black rod, which he pointed at Tammi. It snapped once, a sharp hiss. As Max watched in horror, she looked down for a moment in surprise at the small dart embedded in her thigh, tried to raise the bow again. It was as if she had no strength. She swayed once, suddenly folded like a rag doll, falling face down on the trail, her bow by her side. As Max released Trudie, his hand going for his bow, the man moved with a speed that caught him unawares. He threw what he had been riding to one side, ran down the trail to where Tammi had fallen, scooped her up in his arms. He turned, hoisting her across the shoulder nearest to Max, and sprinted away in the direction from which he had come. Max had his bow drawn now, but dared not shoot, with the movement of the running, and Tammi's back shielding his. By the time he had thought of aiming for the legs, it was too late: the man was a strong runner, and in moments he had disappeared down the trail. The speed at which events had unfolded left Max dazed. Tammi's bow, and the metal device which the man had been riding, lay incongruously on the trail.

Beside him, Trudie spoke, almost inaudibly, shock and horror threading her voice.

"What happened to her?"

Max felt numb.

"He shot her with something."

"He killed her," she said. "Why? Why did he kill her?"

"I think he thought she was going to kill him," he said. The words felt like someone else's, this could not be real. "He saw us, he saw her bow."

She sat down abruptly on the ground, her face pure white, her eyes vacant. Max's thoughts were chaotic as he strove to make sense of what had happened. He walked to the trail, picked up Tammi's bow and quiver, the leather grip still moist from where she had been holding it. He couldn't seem to see clearly. He looked at the device the man had dropped. Beautifully, intricately made from tubes of shining metal, it had large wheels made from fine wire. He could not see it for tears. Half blinded by them, he walked woodenly back to where Trudie sat, absolutely still, her face like a mask. They clung to each other for a moment, both racked by sobs.

"Why did he take her away?"

Her eyes were huge in the pale face, filled with tears and the blankness of shock. Angrily, he wiped his own eyes.

"I don't know. I don't understand." His mind was beginning to clear now. "I don't see why he would take her body. It was just a tiny dart, in her leg." He looked at her, holding both her hands, suddenly seeing it. "Perhaps he used poison. Perhaps it doesn't kill you. Like nightshade. Like snakebite, sometimes."

She got to her feet, desperation in her eyes.

"Come on."

Beyond the rise, beyond the trees, a strange sound had started, a high pitched whistle rising in tone. He jerked her hand.

"We must be careful, Trudie. If we want to help her."

"Come on."

Side by side, they sprinted up the trail. The whistle was deepening into a rasping drone now, beginning to be overlaid by a sound like the wind over rocks. Coming to the edge of the forest, cresting a gentle rise, they stopped momentarily, shocked into immobility by what they saw. Brightly coloured tents stood at the edge of a small meadow, a higher, wooded slope rising beyond. A huge metal thing shaped like a fish, larger than a house, stood on legs in the grass. Atop it, slender dark arms rotated, gathering speed. A wind seemed to be blowing from the thing, tearing at the leaves, blowing grass in their faces. It was starting to make the noise they had heard through the forest, before they came to the lake.

Max could see through the front of it. Two people were sitting there, watching him, dark patches over their eyes. A door in the side stood open, and people were running from the tents. One of them had something over his shoulder, he saw. Tammi. It was Tammi. Bows in their hands, he and Trudie ran out onto the meadow, as the man carrying Tammi passed her in to the metal thing, climbed in himself. Two more people were running from the tents. As they came round the back of the thing, came to the door, Max drew his bow, his eyes slitted against the blast of air, let fly. The arrow found its mark, the figure went down on the grass. As the other person reached out for the first, Trudie's arrow found that one. Two more people jumped out of the machine, pulled the injured two inside. The noise was colossal, deafening now. The thing shifted on its legs, its tail lifting, as the last figure climbed back inside, then, impossibly, it started to rise into the air. Max fired at the people he could see inside, through the transparent front, but his arrow seemed to glance off.

Still rising, the thing floated hugely towards them, almost low enough to touch, the air blasting out from it like a winter storm, beginning to turn to the right as it did so. Teeth gritted, Max fired at its underside, watching his arrow bounce harmlessly off. Beside him, Trudie dropped her bow, screaming at the top of her voice:

"You've killed her! You've taken her from me!"

The thing rose slowly, turning away from them in the direction of the lake. Trudie screamed again, like a wounded animal, desperately, piercingly. The machine's nose seemed to dip, it was as if it hesitated, lurched in the air. Next to Max, Trudie went on screaming, half mad with grief, beating at the air with her fists, as blindingly, shatteringly, something exploded in the middle of his head, pulverising his awareness, smashing him instantly into oblivion.

———————————

She saw the huge thing sway, dip in the air, like a wounded bird struck by an arrow. Half blinded by tears, her mind a sea of grief, she was dimly aware of Max crumpling to the ground beside her, falling face down, his bow half under his body. For a moment the thing recovered, its nose rising again, the downdraught from it blasting the trees at the edge of the clearing as it began to move out over the forest. Then the sound it was making changed slightly, its nose dropped again, and slowly, inexorably, it began to veer to the left, sinking towards the trees. Fixated on it, her vision blurred, she felt disconnected from everything. Then the edge of the spinning disc touched the top of a tree in an explosion of green, there came a shattering noise, and dark fragments flew away from the disc. Abruptly, incredibly, the body of the thing tilted on its side, fell uncontrollably sideways and forwards into the trees, the sound of breaking branches and tearing metal sounding above the other noises. Half visible between the trunks, she saw its dark silhouette crash to the ground, crushing young trees, throwing up a cloud of dust and debris. Suddenly it was very quiet, but for a whistling sound descending the scale. In moments that, too, ceased, leaving only the silence. She could hear her own breathing, tears were running down her face. From the place where the thing had landed, pain, human pain, blasted at her like a wave of heat. She shuddered, her fists clenched, her eyes tightly shut.

For a long moment she stood in the middle of the clearing, shaking, trying to shut out the agony washing out of the forest. Unable to comprehend the immensity of what she felt, what she had just seen, the loss of Tammi, the dawning knowledge that she might have killed Max, she stood as if paralysed, unable to see for her tears. But Tammi had been inside the thing, she had seen them carry her in. This pain, this pain could be hers. From somewhere deep within her the instinct to survive and save welled up, the instinct that had driven her, held her together, since her mother's death. Oblivious to Max lying on the grass beside her, she took a step or two forward. Woodenly, moving as if tranced, she walked towards the edge of the clearing, towards where she had seen the thing come down. She passed into the shade of the trees, coming in moments to the place.

It had smashed an opening in the forest canopy as it came down, and lay on the ground in silence, impossibly still, leaf shadows playing across it. The transparent front and some of the windows in it were broken, she saw, and the spinning arms on top were broken or bent. The body of it had broken its back as it fell, and two people had been thrown out. They lay on the grass in their bright clothes, their limbs at strange angles. The machine creaked a little, a host of tiny, strange noises.

She lowered her barriers for a moment, thinking to search for Tammi's mind, and the pain poured into her like a wave, so that she raised her hands to her head and almost fell, staggering back against a tree. The suffering, always the suffering. Her whole body tensed, trying to shut it out, she moved forward hesitantly, until she was looking down at the two people on the grass. Their clothes were so strange, but they were just people. When she touched them, they were still warm, but they weren't breathing, they were both dead. Somewhere a blackbird was singing. But Tammi was inside, and pain meant life. She looked into the body of the thing, through the gap where it had broken open. Seats remained attached to the floor, but the impact with the ground had crushed one side of the body, and the people lay heaped against it. Even from here she could see the injuries they had suffered when they were thrown against the collapsing metal wall.

She squeezed into the gap, trying to avoid the sharp edges of torn metal. In a moment she stood inside. Somewhere liquid was dripping, a strange, unfamiliar smell in the back of her nose. Numb with shock, she moved forward to where the people lay, their pain burning in her head like hot iron, impossible to fully shut out. Most of them seemed unconscious or dead, but near the open door to the shattered front, she saw a slight movement. It was a man, it wasn't Tammi.

At her feet a tanned, slender hand protruded from under the body of a man, a hand she knew. Bending, she strained to roll the man's body over, onto his back. Tammi lay on top of another person, a woman. Her eyes were closed, and her face wore an expression of peace. Something had cut her cheek, and Trudie bent, gently wiped at the blood with her fingertip. But her neck looked wrong, and when Trudie worked her arm under Tammi's shoulders, bent to lift her, her head lolled loosely, her neck obviously broken. She was still warm, impossibly lifelike, but she had no pulse. The pain, this pain, was not hers.

Trudie picked her up in her arms, cradling her, wrapping her arms around her the way she used to when Tammi fell and hurt herself as a little girl, the way she had after her father raped her, the touch that said I am here, I will protect you, I will feel your pain for you, try to get between you and the world. But the world has found you now, my beautiful little sister, in this crazy, meaningless way, it has broken your neck and killed you. You who could have been whole, you who were not damaged as I am, until I failed you that other time, failed, through my own unforgivable weakness, to put myself between you and him. You who I tried to save with what passes, with me, for love, only to reach out for and kill you, today, in another moment of weakness, because I thought I'd already lost you, and I thought I couldn't go on. And now I have you back, still warm and beautiful in my arms, and I have broken your neck and killed you. I wish there wasn't a cut on your cheek, I wish that you were perfect again. I wish it was me lying dead in your arms, though I know it's never been that way with us, and I don't suppose it would have made things better if it had been.

Her vision awash with tears, she carried Tammi to the hole she had climbed in through. Gently, carefully, she eased her body through, trying to keep it from the jagged metal edges, ignoring the way they cut her own arms and legs, the deep gashes they made. She stood in the sunshine, tears running down her cheeks, her blood running down her skin, looking into her sister's face, at that peace that looked so like sleep. Moving automatically, she carried her away from the wrecked machine, under the trees. Back towards the clearing, out into the sunshine again. Out across the short grass, across to where Max lay. Gently, so gently, she laid Tammi down on the grass next to him, with her face turned up to the sun. The only two she had ever cared about were together again.

She knelt down beside Max, rolled him gently over onto his back. His pulse was as faint as that of a fledgling bird, his breath so shallow that she could hardly feel it on the back of her hand. Whether there was anything left in his mind, whether there would ever be anything left of the person she knew, had thought she loved, she did not know. She sat down beside her sister, and took Max's head into her lap, cradling it in her hands. What little of beauty she had ever touched had come unravelled in her hands, leaving only ashes. This desolation, this destruction, was all there was, all that her power over others had left her. She couldn't seem to stop shaking, her body was racked with sobs. Time must have passed, but it meant nothing.

She did not react at all to the distant drone, overlain by a low thumping sound, that gave hint of its presence over the trees. Did not react at all as it grew in volume, grew into another of the strange machines, growing huge over the trees, banking over the clearing in a fury of sound, the wind blasting down from it, flattening the grass. Did not react at all as it floated down from the sky to land not twenty yards away, as people spilled from it, ran into the forest towards the wreck. Did not react at all as others formed a ring round her, watching her gravely. Only when they tried to take Max from her did she move, and then the grief broke within her, and she fought them like an animal. Some of them held her down while others brought a bag from the machine. They took something from it, then one of them stuck a sharp thing in her arm, and everything ended.

Other books by Rob Turner:-

The Knowing: Book 2 of *Perception*.

Rob Turner studied Natural Sciences at Cambridge, and has worked as a biology teacher and bus driver. He is married with two children, and lives in Cornwall.

https://asgardindustriesdotnet.wordpress.com/

Made in the USA
Charleston, SC
22 January 2017